Everyone Loves Zelda

Romancing the Dog series

Everyone Loves Zelda

Romancing the Dog series

One of three romance novellas
by
Marjorie Pinkerton Miller

SUNACUMEN
PRESS
Colorado Springs, CO

To Chrissy Meyer, the world's best beta-reader

One

THE DAY SHE LEFT PARIS, Julie thought she had the rest of her life figured out.

André would follow her to Seattle as soon as his boss hired his replacement, and they would get married. She would take over her parents' wine shop in the market. She would get Zelda back, and the big dog would live a long and happy life with them.

Some of that worked out. Some of it didn't.

Sitting at their favorite patisserie the morning before her flight, Julie and André kept to the routine they'd developed over the past fourteen months. They held hands, drank espressos, and split a buttery croissant. The only change was the suitcase that sat under their table.

"What time is your flight?" André asked for the tenth time.

Julie rolled her eyes but smiled. "A little after eleven. I need to leave soon."

"I can drive you."

"No. That's silly. Driving in Paris is an exercise in attempted suicide."

"You are not accustomed. Parisians are not so afraid."

"Still, I'll take a cab. You need to get to work. Aren't you working the lunch shift?"

"Yes." André squeezed her hand and paused. His eyes sought hers. "I'll miss you, Julie."

"I'll miss you too, André." She looked at her watch again. "Do you have any news about when you'll be able to come over?"

"I'll get there as soon as I get a visa and they find someone at the restaurant to replace me."

Julie nodded. His answer was always the same.

She stood and threw the long strap of her purse over her head and across her chest. "I should go. I'll text when I get there. It will be too late here to call."

André walked to the door and held it open for her. At the curb, he hailed a taxi and put her bag on the seat next to her. As she ducked in, he leaned forward for a quick kiss.

"*Je t'aime.*"

"I love you too."

Twelve hours later, Julie walked out under the long overhang of the arrivals curb at Seatac and shivered. She'd forgotten about the rain. How could she? She'd lived in Seattle her entire life. She knew it rained from September through June, and yet this dreary drizzle caught her by surprise, and then she felt a wave of nostalgia.

"Yes," she whispered. "This is home."

She took note of the number over the terminal door she'd just exited and texted it to her brother. Just minutes later, he pulled up at the curb in his ancient SUV and jumped out, grinning effusively.

"Hi, big sis! How'd it go?" he asked. "Can we keep you

down on the farm now that you've seen Paree?"

Julie laughed. Of course, he'd say that.

"I'm back, aren't I?" She leaned in for a kiss on the cheek and let Cary put her suitcase in the back for her.

"Did you like it there?" he asked as he pulled out into the traffic lane. "Mom said you got a boyfriend."

"Well, I did meet someone. We're talking about getting married, but he has to come to the U.S. first."

Cary glanced over with his eyebrows pinched.

"But you won't go back, will you?"

"After getting stuck there with the pandemic, I think it will be a while before I want to go overseas again. I got a little homesick."

Taciturn as ever, Cary just nodded and drove north toward the interstate in silence. The rain on the windshield was just heavy enough to require intermittent wiping, and the rhythm lulled Julie into a daze. She shook her head to wake up. She was tired, but it was only two o'clock, and she needed to force herself back onto Pacific time.

"How are things with you, Care Bear?" she asked Cary. "Are you working?"

"I started a new job two weeks ago. So far, so good." He looked at Julie and winked. "But you know that doesn't mean much," he said. Julie nodded. They both knew that it was probably only a matter of time before it wouldn't be "so good."

"Where?"

"An Amazon warehouse in Redmond."

Julie nodded appreciatively. "Good benefits. But hard work, isn't it?"

"Hard work is never my problem. My problem is stupid bosses. So far, this woman seems okay. If she stays out of my face, we'll get along fine."

"But isn't that what bosses do? Get in your face?"

Cary chuckled and nodded. He sped up to pass a truck

that was spraying a cloud of mist at them. "Yeah, that's why I have trouble dealing with them."

"Well, good luck with this one. I know it would make Mom feel a lot better if you stick with it."

"So, what are your plans, sis?"

"First, I'm going to get Zelda from whoever is fostering her. Then, the store. I've got to get back into the swing of things before Mom and Dad retire in a couple of months. And I'll need to hire someone. I can't do it all myself."

"Good luck to you too. I couldn't work for Dad if my life depended on it."

Julie knew that was true. She got along with her father fine. She let him remind her he was boss because he seemed to need to, and she didn't fight it. But for Cary, it had always been a test of wills.

"Well, then, it's a good thing that you haven't had to," she said.

"Was that some kind of a shot?"

As much as he made fun over his inability to hold a job or suffer authority, Cary bristled when others did. She reached over and put her hand on his arm.

"No, little brother. It wasn't. It's not easy to work for your parents. Not for anyone. But probably easier for me than it would be for you. And I love the wine business."

"For that, I'm jealous. You've always known what you wanted to do," Cary said with a wag of his head. "Must be nice."

Julie looked out the window at the familiar passing scenery and wondered if she always knew what she wanted to do, or if she'd always been told. "I'm not so sure about that. But it's a place to start."

Julie left her suitcase inside the door of her apartment without opening it.

"First things first," she told herself.

She pulled her cellphone out of her purse and pulled down her contact list and then her veterinarian's name.

"I'm back!" she announced when Glenda answered.

"Hey, Julie! How was it? Was Paris everything it's supposed to be?"

"Well," Julie paused. How much did she want to reveal about André before he showed up in Seattle? If he never showed up, how embarrassed would she be?

"It was great. I didn't intend to stay so long, but you know what happened."

The noise in Glenda's clinic reminded Julie how busy the place was, so she got to the point.

"I'm ready to pick up Zelda. Can you tell me who is fostering her for me?"

Glenda retrieved the name and number for Julie and read them to her.

"Thanks, Glenda. I appreciate it."

"We should get together so you can tell me all about your trip."

Julie was surprised. "Sure. Maybe we can meet for a cocktail some evening, once I get settled again and figure out how to manage the store."

Julie knew that it was unlikely. She'd taken Zelda to Glenda since she first adopted the big dog, but she and the veterinarian had never become friends.

Immediately after they hung up, Julie dialed the number she got from Glenda. An answering machine picked up, and Julie left a message.

"Hi, Jon. My name is Julie. I got your name and number from Glenda, my vet. She said you are fostering Zelda, my dog. I'm back from France, and I'd like to pick her up sometime soon. Please give me a call. Thanks! Oh, and thanks for taking care of her while I was gone. I hope she wasn't too much trouble."

Two

Julie hung up the wrinkled dress from her suitcase and threw the rest of the clothes she had unpacked into a laundry basket. If she washed the wrinkles out, she could avoid a bunch of ironing.

She closed the empty suitcase and put it in the deepest corner of the closet. She hoped she wouldn't be needing it again for a while. It was good to be home.

Her cellphone buzzed, its tone muted by the comforter on the bed where she'd laid it. The caller ID showed it was the number she had called earlier, looking for Zelda.

"Hello?"

"Hi, this is Jon, the guy who adopted Zelda. I'm returning your call—"

"Oh, thanks for calling back," Julie interrupted. She couldn't contain her excitement over seeing Zelda soon. "Thanks so much for taking care of Zelda. Can I come and get her?"

"As I was trying to say, I'm returning your call as a courtesy. But I can't let you have Zelda. She's my dog now."

Julie twirled and sat down on the bed hard. She shook her head.

"No. She's my dog," she said, trying to keep her voice calm. "The vet asked you to foster her, not adopt her."

"But you've been gone more than a year. What did you expect?"

"I didn't expect to be gone so long."

"Well, you were. Zelda's been with me too long now," he said, his voice stern. "You have to let her go."

Julie took a deep breath, her heart pounding. This couldn't be happening!

"Look. I'm sorry. I expected to be gone only a few months."

"So, what happened?"

Julie hesitated. Did she have to explain herself to this man intent on stealing her dog? If that's what it took, she decided, she would.

"Well, I took an apprenticeship with a sommelier in Paris to learn French wines. My parents own a wine store here, and I expect to take it over soon. They thought it would be great experience for me to go overseas and see if I could pick up some wine smarts. I was only going to be gone for six months."

"So why the year?"

"And when the pandemic hit, I couldn't come home. So I ended up hanging out longer."

Jon made a dismissive snort. "I hope you had a great time. But Zelda is mine now. I can't give her up."

"But you agreed to foster." Julie heard the whine in her voice and lowered it. "That means you give up the dog when the owner returns."

Jon paused; perhaps he was considering her logic.

"Yes, I was going to foster," he said instead. "But hear

me out. My dog died from cancer just two months after he and I got back from Iraq. We had been there together for four years. I missed Milo so much I was afraid to give my heart to another dog. My vet—Glenda, I guess you know her—asked if I'd foster Zelda. I didn't know how attached we were going to get. And Glenda said it would only be a few months. But it was more than a year."

The story disarmed Julie. "Uh, well ... thanks for your service. I think military dogs are so great. But I love Zelda. I've missed her so much. And she's mine. I didn't plan the pandemic."

Jon chuckled. "No one did. But if I remember right, people have been coming back from Europe all the time."

Julie tried to rein in her anger. She was getting impatient with this conversation. There was no question. Zelda was hers; always was and always would be.

"Yes, I suppose some people found a way to come back. But I had another reason to stay."

"What was that?"

"It's really none of your business."

"Not much of an argument."

"Okay." Julie exhaled with exasperation. Who was this Jon and why did he think he had the right to hear her explanation? Whether she had one or not didn't change the fact that Zelda was her dog. "His name is André."

Now Jon laughed. "What? Who's André?"

"The man I fell in love with."

"Ohhhhhh." His tone was condescending. "Oh, now it's making sense. And where is André now?"

"Back in France. He's waiting to get a visa so he can come here. We plan to get married."

"Oh. Then I think you should wait till André gets here and you guys can go and get another dog. The way I see it, you traded Zelda for André. And now you're not happy with the bargain."

Julie was getting frantic. She didn't expect any debate, and this argument was going on far too long. Perhaps if she pretended to compromise, she could get Zelda back.

"Please. You have to at least let me see her. You'll see how much she loves me."

Jon was stern again. "I don't think so."

"Why not?"

"It will just confuse her."

"Oh, come on. Dogs don't register 'confused.'"

"Shows how little you know about dogs. Or Zelda."

"Please." She switched to pathetic pleading. "I had Zelda for three years before you got her. You've only had her for a year."

"Fourteen months."

"Whatever. Please!"

Jon hesitated for a moment, and Julie started to hope he'd relent.

"I'm sorry, but this conversation is over," he said instead. "And don't you try to stalk us. I'll call the police."

The line disconnected. Julie stared at the phone in disbelief and lay back on her bed, her face in her hands.

"Wow. What a jerk!"

Julie accepted her mother's invitation to dinner that evening. She hadn't had a chance to stock up on groceries, and she was too distraught over Zelda to sit in a public restaurant.

She found her mother in the kitchen of her childhood home and gave her a big hug.

"I'm so happy you're finally home," her mother cried, her arms around Julie. "Did you feel trapped?"

"I had my moments, my panic attacks, but André helped. If it hadn't been for him, I would probably have figured out a way to get back sooner."

"Well, your dad and I wished you had."

"Yes, but André and I wouldn't be engaged if I'd come home right away." Julie thought her reasoning was sound until she said it out loud. Her mother reached over and grabbed Julie's left hand and lifted it into the air for inspection.

"Engaged, huh?" Her mother sniffed. "I don't see a ring. Or don't they do that over there?"

Julie pulled her hand back. "We decided to get married right before I left. He didn't have time. Anyway, rings, diamonds. Whatever. You don't need them to get engaged."

"You'll have plenty on your mind for the next few weeks as your dad and I retire and head for Alaska." Her mother gave a dismissive wave and turned back to the loaf of bread she was slicing. "So, if it takes André a while to get here, that might be for the best. You should go say hi to your dad. He's in the TV room with Cary."

A few minutes later, Julie rejoined her mother in the kitchen to help her bring the food to the dining room table. As they set the dishes down, Cary and her father pulled out their chairs and sat.

Such an American scene, Julie thought. She'd missed these family dinners, even though at one time, she'd been impatient with their routine. She picked up the wine bottle from the buffet and filled their glasses before sitting down.

"Have you gone to get Zelda yet?" her mother asked as she started passing the dishes around. "You could have brought her here, you know. We've missed her so much."

Julie fought back a sudden rush of tears—tears that she'd held back all afternoon, nurturing her anger with the man who held Zelda captive instead.

"I don't know what to do." She sniffed and stood up to grab a Kleenex off the dining room bureau. "The guy who fostered her won't tell me where he lives, and he won't give her back. He says she's his now."

Cary threw up his hands theatrically. "But wasn't he

just supposed to foster her until you came back?"

"Yes! I called him but he said he won't give her up," Julie said. "He said I was gone too long."

"Did you explain the situation?" her mother asked.

Exasperated at the obvious answer, Julie retorted a bit more strongly than she intended. "Yes, of course I did. But he said he had lost his dog and didn't think he wanted a new one right away. He didn't think he'd ever love another dog. But you know, everyone loves Zelda."

"Just go get a new dog," her father said. He appeared more focused on choosing just the right pieces of chicken off the platter than on the conversation. "There's lots of them in the pound who need homes. That's where you found Zelda."

Julie, her mother, and Cary all stopped what they were doing and looked at him with disbelief. Had he just suggested group suicide, it would have shocked them no more. Her father felt the tension and looked up.

"What? What did I say?" he asked, looking from one to the other. He received three disgusted looks but no answer.

Julie's mother shook her head. "Pay no attention to him. He's never understood dogs. Why don't I ask my sister if there isn't some law?"

"Mom, I can't afford to bring a lawyer into this. I'll figure this out—"

Cary cut her off. "I'll steal her for you. I'll figure out where he lives, and I'll case the joint and when he's not there, I'll grab her."

Their mother pointed her fork menacingly at him.

"Cary, you're not going to risk another misdemeanor over this. I thought you'd turned over a new leaf."

Cary looked sheepish. "I'm just trying to help." He held up his glass of wine, as if in atonement. "By the way, Mom, this is pretty good. Is it Willamette Valley pinot?"

"Yes. Good guess." His mother seemed pleased.

"It's not a guess, Mom. I have a pretty good palate, thanks to you." He tipped his glass at her.

"Ha! Look at you. So sophisticated all the sudden," Julie said, laughing and slugging him in the shoulder.

"Mom made me do all the wine tastings while you were gone," Cary explained. "I guess she thought I was handsome enough to pull it off."

He leaned over to Julie and pretended to share something confidential. "And, I'll tell you. It was a pretty good gig. Lots of really nice young women come to wine tastings."

"Fun, fun, fun," his father mocked. "That's all you think about, Cary. The wine business isn't about pretty young women."

He turned to Julie. "Forget the dog, dear. You need to concentrate now on catching up at the store. Your mom and I expect to retire in three weeks."

"I will, Dad, but I love Zelda, and I have to get her back first."

Cary interjected. "My offer remains."

"Shut up, dummy," Julie said. "We're not going to commit a felony together. I'll figure something out."

"Back to the store," her father said. "Are you coming in tomorrow?"

Three

"THREE MAISON BLEUE FRONTIERE SYRAH, 2017," Julie called out from where she kneeled in front of the bottom shelf of a rack of wine. "And one Graviere Syrah, also 2017."

Her mother checked the bottles off on the list. She held the clipboard in one hand and a pen in the other and let her arms fall to the side. She shook her shoulders to loosen the strain from the second full day of taking inventory.

"Boy, this is tiring," she said, exhaling a big breath. "I don't remember it ever being this hard."

"Well, it is the first time you're doing inventory at age 65," Julie said. There was no compassion in her voice.

"I did it at 64."

"So now you're a year older. Let's start on cabs."

Julie's mother stared at her daughter and shook her head. "No, let's take a break."

Julie hoisted herself up on one of the stools they kept behind the checkout counter and pouted while her mother went into the back to get a cup of coffee and returned.

"What's with you today? I used to count on a little enthusiasm from you. I may be cranky because I'm old and tired, but you don't have an excuse."

Julie shrugged and didn't answer. She stared into the distance, out the big store windows to the street. The rain had stopped, but it was still a dreary mid-50s, one of those June days that seemed to portend that summer would never come.

"Chin up, girl," her mother said, pulling herself onto the stool next to Julie. "You seem so sad. No luck with Zelda yet?"

Julie shook her head. "I haven't figured anything out yet. I called Glenda back and she said she'd talk to Jon."

"Who?"

"The guy who has Zelda. And meanwhile, I've been too busy trying to get my new phone and cable set up and restarting mail and stuff. But I plan to do nothing this weekend but work on getting her back."

"Aren't you going to work on Saturday?"

"Mom, I really have to do something. If I had any inkling I had lost Zelda, I'm not sure I would have come back."

"Did Glenda have any ideas?" Her mother sipped her coffee noisily, adding to Julie's irritation.

"No, and she wouldn't give me Jon's address. She said it violated privacy rules." Julie leaned forward on her elbows and hid her face in her hands.

"You weren't planning to take Cary up on his offer to steal her, were you?"

"No, but I thought if I could stop by he would see how much Zelda loves me, maybe it would change things. And I tried texting him, but he hasn't responded."

"Well, perhaps your dad is right. Maybe you should just find another Zelda. You can't be such a sad sack when André gets here or he'll wonder why he came."

Julie's phone rang, and she glanced at the caller ID. Her face brightened.

"I'm going to go in the back to get this. It's André. I've been calling and texting him, but I couldn't get through."

"Sure, dear."

Julie pushed through the swinging door to the warehouse and office space in back of the store.

"André!"

"*Mi amor*! I see your text. Is everything good there? Your flight was okay?"

"Yes, but I miss you André. I can't wait for you to get here. Do you have any idea when you can come?"

"You must be patient, *mi amor*. Jacque is looking for a new sous chef to replace me. As soon as he finds one, I'll get my ticket and come." André was calling from Paris, but the reception was so clear it made Julie's heart ache. He sounded like he was next door.

"So you got your visa?" she asked.

"Turns out, I don't need a visa yet. I just have to pack and get my ticket."

"But you can do that now, right?"

"But no hurry. I'll do it as soon as I know when I can leave."

"You are coming, aren't you?"

Julie knew she sounded desperate. Her apartment felt empty and sullen with the constant drizzle and the absence of Zelda.

"*Oui, petite*! I will call you as soon as I make plans. How are your parents?"

"Fine. They want to meet you. I hope you get here before they leave on their sailboat."

"And I want to meet them. But I must go now. Jacque has me closing the restaurant tonight, but I wanted to catch you while I could."

"I'm so glad you called—"

"*Bientot!*" he said, not waiting for her to finish. "*Ciao!*" The line disconnected.

Julie let the hand that held the phone drop to her side and walked back into the front of the store.

"You don't look happy, my dear," her mother said.

"Sometimes I wonder if André is really coming. He doesn't seem to be in much of a hurry."

"It's a big change, honey. Give him some time. Maybe he has things to work out before he leaves. Now, we need to get to work. If we're going to sign this store over to you, we need to get this inventory done and finish the rest of the paperwork. Your father's eager to get on the boat. You know he's been wanting to sail to Alaska forever."

"Alaska's not going anywhere, Mom."

"Yes, but we can't go if we aren't out of here by the end of June. We can't sail in the winter, you know."

Julie sighed. "Yes, let's get back to it." Julie locked her fingers behind her back and stretched her arms out, her chest thrust forward. "The sooner we finish this miserable task, the happier we'll both be."

Julie met André at the restaurant in Paris where she was studying under the sommelier in the dining room and he was working in the kitchen as a sous chef.

At first, she barely noticed him—just another young, pretty French man in tight pants and a stark, asymmetrical haircut that looked like it was meant to communicate edginess and trendy-restaurant *savoir faire.* She actually snorted to herself derisively the first time she saw him across the serving counter.

"What's that mean?" the sommalier asked.

Julie was embarrassed that he had overheard her.

"*Rien,*" she said, shaking her head. "Just a little sinus problem."

"*Vraiment?*" he asked, smiling as if he agreed with her

assessment. He nodded at André. "He might be a bit of a dandy, but he's going places. Chef thinks he'll be famous one day."

Working until close at a restaurant is a recipe for tryst-building in Paris, as it is anywhere, Julie soon learned. The staff sat on the high stainless-steel tables in the kitchen into the early morning, draining bottles of Champagne and fine wine, munching on leftovers from the evening's specials. Only the most dedicated bachelors and single women and a few married employees avoided some kind of entanglement for long.

At first, Julie was able to keep her romance with André hidden, but another truism of the restaurant business is how hard it is to keep secrets. Everyone knew everyone else's business, whether financial, romantic, or familial.

When her six-month stay was extended by the pandemic, their affair was just starting to heat up. The virus and the difficulty of travel gave her an excuse to postpone her return again and again. But eventually, the excuses wore out, as did her patience with all things French. She was homesick and she missed Zelda.

Just before she left for Seattle, André's indifference to their seperation suddenly morphed into a sorrow he could not abide. He proposed marriage. Surprised, Julie took a few days to try to figure out what had happened between them, examine his motives, and to consider the idea. But, enchanted by the idea of bringing home a successful, good-looking fiancé, she shed her suspicions and said yes.

JULIE STEPPED OFF THE BUS and turned to walk up the hill. It was only a couple of blocks to her apartment building, but in her mood, the incline felt like Mount Everest. Head down, she wondered how much of her exhaustion was due to jet lag and how much was due to everything that had gone wrong since she got back.

She had tried to talk her parents into digitizing their inventory and computerizing their business systems for the past two years, but they weren't interested. Now they were trudging through their usual two weeks of annual inventory with pencil and paper, and she had another two weeks of entering the information onto an old Excel spreadsheet that was her mother's idea of modern bookkeeping. André seemed to be stalling when it came to following her to Seattle, and so far, she'd had no luck in getting Jon to pay attention to her pleas for Zelda.

Looking up before crossing the street, she noticed a man walking ahead of her, heading up the same hill, with a dog that looked just like Zelda—a big brown, black, and white Australian Shepherd mix. Was she going crazy? Was every dog going to look to her like Zelda from now on?

She ran ahead, gaining on them until she was sure it wasn't an illusion. It was Zelda. It had to be.

"Zelda!" she yelled. "Is that you, Zelda?!"

The dog stopped and turned. In less than a second, Zelda recognized Julie and started barking. She pulled on her leash and yanked it out of the man's hand.

Too late, he turned to catch Zelda, but she was too fast. Julie put down her grocery bag and purse and knelt down, anticipating all 80 pounds of Zelda crashing into her. She knew how easy it was for Zelda to knock a person over.

"Oh my god, Zelda!" Julie cried as the dog nuzzled her and pranced in her hug. "I was so worried. I thought I'd never see you again!" Tears ran down her face, and Zelda lapped them up with her big tongue.

The man walked back toward them and stood a few paces away. Julie looked up at him with Zelda still wiggling in her embrace.

"You must be Jon. See? See how much she loves me?"

Jon stood and watched for a long minute. Finally, as Zelda started to settle down, he called, "Zelda! Come here!"

Zelda waddled over to him, still dancing from happiness, and Jon picked up the end of her leash. Julie stood, brushed off the knees of her jeans, and picked up her purse and groceries.

"Don't tell me," he said, a snarl in his voice. "You are Julie. You're stalking me. I told you I'd call—"

Julie held out her free hand. "No! I wasn't stalking you. I was walking home." She pointed to her apartment building a hundred yards ahead. "I live right there!"

"Where?" he said, spinning around to see where she was pointing. "In my building?"

"I don't know what building is yours. Honest. I'm not stalking you! I live in 1256. Do you?" She wiped her face with the back of her hand, but the tears still fell.

Jon turned back to her, his frown gone. Replacing it was a sheepish grin. "Yeah. I do. I guess we're neighbors."

Zelda pulled Jon back toward Julie, still wiggling with excitement. It would have taken a zombie, Julie thought, to not see how much Zelda loved her. The dog nuzzled her head between Julie's knees, and Julie bent down to scratch her head with her free hand.

"Oh, Zelda," she said through her tears. "I missed you so much! Will you ever forgive me?"

"Well, this is unfortunate," Jon said. He didn't seem as oblivious to Julie and Zelda's happiness as he was irritated by it.

"Why would you say that? I think it's serendipity!"

Jon shook his head and looked away.

"We have to talk," Julie said, finally gaining control over the waterworks on her face. "Look, it's clear that Zelda missed me. If you really love her like you say, you wouldn't want her to be hurt, would you?"

Jon turned back to face her. "Why? You say you love her and you left. That probably hurt her."

"Come on, Jon. We have to talk about this seriously.

Let's pick some neutral territory and figure this out. I don't want to have to call a lawyer or something."

Jon laughed at that with an exuberance that confused Julie. Why would that be so funny?

"A lawyer, huh?" he said.

"Oh, please, don't make me do it that way. We don't need to make this a supreme court case, do we? Can't I at least see her some until we get this worked out?"

Jon's laughter stopped and for the first time, he seemed to take a good look at Julie. She wiped the last of her tears away and returned his stare. He was handsome in a boyish kind of way. She had trouble placing his age, but his full lips, freckles, and long red curls probably made him look much younger than he was.

His steady gaze didn't bother her. Julie knew she was pretty. Even if her mascara and eyeliner were now smudged or streaming down her cheeks, she had a face like the girls next door of the 1950s movies. She knew it disarmed men, and she tried not to take advantage of it when it wasn't necessary.

Now it seemed necessary, and she smiled at him charmingly and reached up to fluff the curls of her long, brunette hair. An involuntary smile crept across his face, and he turned away, as if to make it stop.

"Okay. I can see how much you mean to her. Maybe we can go for a walk with her sometime. We can talk this over."

"Great. That's great." Julie wanted to sound grateful, but Zelda was her dog, and she shouldn't need to beg for a chance to see her. Still, this was progress.

"How about in the park around the corner? Tomorrow morning?" he asked.

Julie didn't want to sound pushy, but she needed to nail down his commitment before he disappeared behind his apartment door with Zelda. "How about tonight? Why not now?"

Jon shook his head. "I'm sorry I have company for dinner tonight. A nice woman who I'm happy to say likes Zelda very much."

Horror swept across Julie's face.

"You're not considering another mom for Zelda, are you? That's just—"

Jon chuckled at her desperation. "Well, I haven't proposed or anything. We just met two weeks ago."

"Well, good," Julie said, relieved. "I could watch Zelda while you guys have dinner tonight."

Jon shook his head and turned to continue up the walk.

"She *is* my dog, you know," Julie called after him.

"I'm not so sure. Isn't possession nine-tenths of the law?"

"Not when it comes to kids and dogs."

Jon turned again, smiling broadly at that. "You just made that up."

"No." She tried to look serious, but his smile was contagious. "Yes. But okay. Park tomorrow morning. How about six?"

"Most nights I work until two. Two a.m., that is. Six isn't in my wheelhouse. Can we do it later?"

Julie scrambled. She needed to make her case as soon as possible. What if Jon moved away? Or his new girlfriend took Zelda to keep her from Julie.

"Well, I've got to go to work at nine. But, how about noon? I'll try to get away from the store for an hour."

Jon nodded. Clearly, she wasn't going to give up. "Okay. Noon it is. We'll see you there. Say goodbye, Zelda."

He turned again to walk away, and Julie laughed and caught up with them.

"I'm walking with you, you know. We live in the same building. You can't get away from me that easy."

Four

The next noon, Julie walked to the park from the bus stop, her arm hooked through her brother's. Cary spotted Jon and Zelda first and pulled them in the right direction. Julie waved and Zelda turned toward them, wiggling with excitement.

As they drew near, Cary stuck out a hand to shake.

"Hi, I'm Cary."

Jon looked confused and stood back. "Another boyfriend? Didn't she trust me?"

He turned to Julie. "And what does André think of this?"

"No," Julie said, surprised that he remembered André's name. "Cary's my brother. Moral support. The boyfriend is in France, remember?"

Jon looked Cary over as if he were evaluating him for a job. He smiled, perhaps having decided Cary was a suitable uncle for Zelda.

"Yeah, well, nice to meet you," Jon said, finally accepting the handshake.

"Cary misses Zelda, too," Julie said. "He wanted to come along."

"What do you do, Cary, that you have noon hours free?"

"Amazon," Cary said simply.

"Oh, what department? I know some folks there."

"Warehouse. Night shift."

"Oh." Jon looked embarrassed, as if he'd expected an entirely different answer. "Let's walk, shall we? I usually take Zelda for a long one in the morning and again before I head off for work. But I made an exception for today."

Jon turned to walk down the path, and Julie fell in step. "And where do you work?" she asked, reaching over for Zelda's leash. Jon relinquished it without resistance.

"Bin 409. Bartender. And you?"

"I'm taking over my parents' wine store in a month. I'm usually working from nine to five. No lunch. But Mom's covering for me today."

They came to a fork in the path, and Zelda led them down the narrow choice on the left. Apparently, it was her new routine. Julie and Zelda stepped ahead, and Cary and Jon walked behind them.

"So, you're a bartender," Cary said.

"Well, yes. For now."

"Maybe it's something I should get into. How long have you been doing it? Forever?"

Jon laughed. "I'm not that old."

Julie turned to judge for herself. Until then, she hadn't focused on Jon's relative age. He looked older than she did, but not by much.

"I've been bartending since I got back from Iraq," Jon elaborated. "I'm in law school during the day—mostly online classes now. From home. I want to practice family law."

"You were in Iraq?" Cary sounded impressed. "Wow,

remind me never to introduce you to my parents. They already think I'm a slacker. They'll meet you and probably want to adopt you."

Julie heard the awe in Cary's voice. Was this emergent bromance going to turn her brother against her? Would he now argue that Jon should get Zelda?

Jon laughed at Cary's ebullience. "Well, I doubt that. So are you here to convince me to give up Zelda?"

Julie turned to see how Cary would respond.

He was shaking his head. "Like Julie said, 'moral support.' And you don't realize how much our family loves Zelda. I wanted to see her again too."

Jon's face turned sour. "Of course. But Zelda is mine now. I've had her for more than a year. I lost my dog—"

"Yes, Julie told us," Cary interrupted. "Your dog had cancer. I'm sorry."

That tamped down the camaraderie a bit, and they all walked in silence. Julie pulled Zelda to a stop at a point where the trail tracked close to the edge of a cliff overlooking Puget Sound. She squatted down and put her arm around her big dog. Zelda wiggled closer, snuggling her back.

"Look at that," Cary said, pointing at them. "How can you—"

"... break them up?" Jon completed his thought. "It was her decision. She's the one who left."

Julie's eyes started to burn with developing tears. "I didn't..." She wanted to argue, but her throat tightened, and she couldn't get another word out.

Cary came to her rescue. "Can I make a suggestion?"

"Sure," Jon said. "As long as it doesn't mean I give up Zelda."

Julie stood and frowned at Cary. Was he going to sabotage her?

"You work at night, right?" Cary asked Jon. "And you

study at home in the day. You go to work at what, six? Seven?"

"Six." Jon sounded as skeptical as Julie felt.

But Cary continued. "And when you work at night you don't get home until when? Two?"

"Yes. About that."

Cary nodded. "And you take Zelda out that late?"

"When I'm not too tired."

Cary shook his head, as if disgusted. "And if you are too tired?"

"She has to wait until morning," Jon admitted, grimacing.

Cary turned to Julie. "And you work all day at the store. Right?"

She nodded.

Cary clasped his hands in front of him, like he'd figured it all out. "So, how about this?"

He paused, and Julie kicked him lightly in the shin. "Get on with it, brother," she urged.

"Jon will keep Zelda during the day while he's home studying. One or both of you can walk her at five. Jon hands her off to Julie before he goes to work. Zelda stays with Jules overnight. Next morning, Jules can drop her off at Jon's place after their walk and before she leaves for work. You split vet bills, license fees. Everything."

Julie stared at Cary. She wasn't sure she loved the idea. But she had to give him credit: it made sense.

Cary held out his hands to his sides and looked back and forth at them. "No brainer, don't you think?"

Julie looked at Jon. Was he going to budge first or was she?

"Come on. You live in the same building. Easy peasy!" Cary exclaimed.

"But is she mine or Jon's, Cary?" Julie asked.

Cary raised his arms higher. "Does a dog really belong

to anyone? A dog isn't a thing. It isn't a possession. A dog is love. And you both love her. It actually solves a problem for both of you. Do you know how much doggie day-care costs?"

Julie shook her head in wonder. How did Cary get so smart? Why was he pretending to be such a slacker when he clearly had talents?

She turned to Jon. "What do you think? At least in the short term, it seems like an idea. Then once you get your law degree, I guess you can figure out the legal answer."

Jon studied Julie's face, as if he were noticing for the first time how much he liked it. He looked away and shrugged. "Okay. Let's give it a try. How about three months. See if it works."

Quickly, Julie stuck out her hand to seal the deal. Jon smiled, as if in spite of himself, and shook his head. He clasped her hand and held it. He looked over at Cary. "Remind me when I get a job as a lawyer to hire you as a negotiator. You're a natural."

Cary grinned. "Years of having to talk my way out of trouble."

Zelda stood up and shook herself, perhaps sensing something had been settled and it was time to go back to Jon's apartment for a nap. The humans turned around and Julie handed Jon the leash.

"Your turn," she said, winking at him. She slipped back to walk beside Cary and patted him on the back.

"You're really too smart to be working in a warehouse, you know."

"I know," he said. "Maybe someday I'll turn things around. Don't give up on me."

A WEEK LATER, JULIE STOOD at the front of the elevator, impatient for the door to open. She was late again. As the doors opened and she ran down the hallway toward Jon's apartment, she saw Jon hooking up Zelda's leash outside his apartment door. He stood up, leash in hand.

"Julie, this is the third time this week that you've been late," he scolded her. "This new plan isn't going to work if you don't do your part. You have to get here on time."

Julie had run from the bus to the apartment building, and now she was breathless.

"I swear … Jon … it will get better." She huffed, trying to catch her breath. "Once I get Mom and Dad out of the picture and can hire some help, I won't have to run like this."

Jon didn't look convinced.

"I'm sorry, really I am," she insisted.

Jon shook his head in disgust, and together they walked to the elevator and waited in silence, Julie still catching her breath.

The elevator opened and they stepped inside.

"I know this might be a bad time to talk about this, but …" Julie started, then stopped. She looked over at Jon, who stared straight ahead. A "bad time" might have been an understatement, she realized.

"You know, there's something about the way people say 'but … ,'" he said.

Julie faked a little laugh. Humor him, she thought.

"Yes, I know what you mean. But I've been meaning to ask you what you feed Zelda. I think we should agree on a diet for her."

Jon raised his eyebrows and finally met her eye.

"A diet? You think she's fat?"

Julie shook her head. "I don't mean *diet* diet. I mean we should agree on what kind of food she should eat and when. And yes, she is a little overweight. Big dogs have enough problems with their joints. They don't need to carry extra weight."

The elevator door opened, and they walked out onto

the street, Julie still carrying the purse she took to work.

"So what do you recommend?" Jon asked, snarkily. "I suppose you have some high-end, gourmet, available-only-at-the-vet brand in mind."

Julie didn't like his tone. "Look. If keeping Zelda half-time is above your budget, just let me know. I'll be glad to take over full-time."

"Oh, so this is another ploy to try to steal her from me."

This conversation wasn't going well. Perhaps the day she came home late wasn't the time to raise the issue. But it wasn't her fault. With her parents focused on retiring and getting out of town, she was shouldering more and more of the responsibility at the store, and so far she hadn't found an employee to help.

Still, Jon's attitude pissed her off. "Steal her? You stole her from me, remember?"

"Might I remind you, that is an unsettled debate," Jon said, setting a quick pace down the park path with Zelda leading. "Let's get back to the diet thing."

"Well, cost shouldn't be an issue," Julie said. "If you were feeding her before, and now you only have to buy half as much food, you should be able to pay for something better than that low-grade chow you've been feeding her."

Jon took a deep breath, indicating that he, too, was trying to keep his cool. He was nearly grimacing, and Julie wondered what had gone poorly for him that day. He looked uncomfortable and impatient.

"Let's cut to the chase, Julie. What do you want me to feed her?" He sounded like he couldn't wait to get to work and end this exchange.

"How about if I buy the food, and I'll just let you know what half of the bill is," Julie offered. "You can pay me as we go along."

"Fine. End of discussion, okay?"

Julie signed audibly and involuntarily.

"What? What was that all about?" Jon said, laughing. Somehow he seemed to have recovered his sense of humor.

"It was so much easier when it was just me and Zellie."

Jon looked over and smiled. "But back then, you weren't taking over a wine store. Look," he said, "I think Cary was right. I think if we can get this figured out, it will be best for all of us. Especially Zelda."

Julie met his eyes. He was a decent guy, she realized. Maybe she was lucky that it was Jon who had fostered Zelda. Maybe everything would work out for the best.

Five

Julie scrambled out of the elevator and ran down the hall, looking at her watch. Late again.

Jon had not been happy the day before, and she had promised to get to the apartment on time. He was going to be furious.

She knocked on the door and held her breath. Would he threaten to take Zelda away from her again? She waited. No answer. She knocked again. Finally, she gave up and took the stairs up one flight to her own floor. As she unlocked her door, she glanced at her phone to see a text from Jon:

> We couldn't wait any longer. Perhaps you should reconsider your commitment.

She groaned. Obviously, Jon didn't understand the pressure she was under trying to get her parents out of the store and off on their retirement. Every time she thought things were copacetic and they were ready, her mother came up with more issues they needed to settle; more reorganization that needed done. And some days, her mother was late showing up for the short evening shift because she was tied up with packing and getting the house ready to rent out.

Inside her apartment, Julie laid her purse down and reached in the refrigerator for a bottle of wine she'd opened the night before. If things kept going this way, her self-medicating with wine would put ten pounds on her petite frame.

Before she finished extracting the cork she'd wedged into the bottle, she heard the knock on the door. No mystery who that was.

Jon stood outside with Zelda on her leash. Zelda pushed past them both and ran into the living room to find an old chew toy. She settled down, clearly unconcerned with Julie's tardiness. Before Jon could complain, Julie apologized.

"I know I was late. It's just getting really hard to get out of the store. Mom is covering evenings, but I can't leave until she gets there."

"We had a nice walk. Thanks for asking." Jon's smile was more of a smirk than a grin.

"I promise things will be better once Mom and Dad are out of there and I can hire someone."

"Sure," Jon said, turning away. "I've got to get to work. I can see you're busy."

"But you can't take her away from me," Julie said, expecting an argument. "I'll work this out."

Jon turned back and held up a palm. "Calm down, Julie. I'm not going to take her away from you. I've got to go now, but we can talk tomorrow."

"Okay. I'll be here on time. I promise."

Jon leaned past her and waved at Zelda. "Bye, girl. See you, Julie."

Zelda hopped up and joined Julie at the door. They watched Jon walk down the hallway toward the elevator. As the bell dinged and the door opened, he turned to look back at them. Julie ducked inside and closed her door.

"We don't want him to think we were mooning over him, do we?" she asked Zelda. Julie laughed as the dog shook vigorously as if agreeing and returned to her chew toy.

The next evening at the store, Julie's mom came rushing in, and Julie greeted her, relieved. "Thanks for coming in early, Mom."

"What's the urgency?" her mother asked as she put her purse away and checked her hair in the mirror behind the counter. "Big plans tonight?"

"No, I've just been late for the walk with Zelda and Jon twice this week. I'm afraid he's going to use this as proof that I don't have time for her."

"I don't think he's going to do that," her mother said, strangely confident.

"How do you know?"

"From what Cary says, he doesn't seem like that kind of guy."

Julie folded up the rag she was using as a dust cloth and stuck it under the counter. "Cary?" she asked. "Cary hates everyone. You mean he said he likes Jon?"

"Well, not romantic likes. He said he seemed reasonable."

"Cary likes reasonable? Boy, he has changed! I was only gone a year!"

"Well, he hasn't changed that much. But he liked the fact that Jon had been in Iraq."

"Which is odd, too," Julie said, gathering her purse and her keys for a quick exit. "Cary's never had much affinity for the military."

"Ah, Cary the enigma. Who knows what he's seen on TV lately? Anyway, you go ahead. Meet with Jon. Figure something out. You need to get things cleared up before your dad and I leave for Alaska."

It was misting at five o'clock when Jon and Julie walked Zelda to the park. Zelda was wrapped tightly in a doggie raincoat—one Julie had never seen before.

"Where'd you get the raincoat?" she asked.

"The pet store down the street by Whole Foods."

"Does she like it?"

"She seems indifferent to it once we start walking, but she always argues a bit when I put it on her."

Glad to put off a discussion of her tardiness, Julie told him about the time she tried to get Zelda to wear booties. "It had rained about 90 days straight, and I was trying to keep the floors cleaner, you know. But once I got them on her—that wasn't easy!—she wouldn't walk. She just stood there trying to figure out how to get all four feet off the ground at one time. It was pretty funny. I decided it wasn't worth the angst it was causing her."

Jon said nothing. He didn't even chuckle.

Uh-oh, Julie thought. Here it comes. The "talk."

"Any trouble getting off early today?" he asked.

Julie took a deep breath before she answered. "No. But I can't ask Mom to come in early every day. They're trying to wrap things up here and get ready to head to Alaska on their boat."

"So what are we going to do? I have to be at the bar five days a week at six. I can't wait for you."

Julie frowned. "Yeah, I understand. And it's likely to get harder for me to leave when I get a new employee. I'll probably need to be there until we close at seven every night."

"Right, so I've been thinking," Jon said. His tone was more conciliatory than she expected. "Why don't I walk her at four or five every afternoon, and then leave her in your apartment? She'll be here when you get home and you can walk her before bedtime. Of course, you'd have to trust me with a key to your place."

Julie was surprised. She had expected this problem would lead to more of an argument about who was best situated to keep Zelda—full-time. Instead, he was offering an easy and reasonable compromise.

"Well, it's not like I don't know where to find you," she said, trying not to sound too eager. "I guess that would be okay. It would take the stress out of trying to coordinate our schedules every day."

Jon looked over at her, his eyes smiling like he read right through her nonchalance. "So, it's a deal?"

Julie nodded. "Yes, I'll go to the hardware store tonight. I'll drop the key off at your apartment later. I can put it under the door."

"No, tonight's my night off. I'll keep Zelda until then. Just come by when you get it, and you can take her home then."

Julie skipped a little step and then tried to drag her feet. Why was she so afraid of admitting she was coming to like Jon so much? Not only was he reasonable and sympathetic, he was good looking, ambitious, and smart. But while he had shown a willingness to work with her to solve the Zelda problem, he hadn't indicated anything more than a platonic interest in her as Zelda's mom.

Which was for the best, Julie admitted to herself as they walked the rest of the park circuit in silence. André was likely to show up on her doorstep soon, and her fascination with Jon would recede.

Six

Two hours later, Jon opened his apartment door and stepped aside to admit Julie. Zelda got up and sauntered over for an ear scratch. Clearly she was comfortable here.

Jon's apartment was clean and neat. No groceries on the kitchen counter or dirty dishes in the sink. The tile floors shone, reflecting the ceiling lights. Beyond the kitchen, the walls were bare, devoid of artwork or posters. A large desk piled high with law books sat in the far end of the living room, and a couple of La-Z-Boys, a small end table, and a tiny TV on a hand-me-down table filled out the space.

"I guess you can see I haven't had much time to decorate," Jon said apologetically.

"It's *so* clean though," she said. "Where's the dog hair? I have dog hair everywhere!"

Jon laughed and grinned shyly. "Yeah, you caught me. I just vacuumed. Didn't want you to think I don't know how to house a dog."

Julie handed him the little envelope with the apartment key she had just had made at the Ace. "Here's the key. The lock is a bit sticky, just so you know. You have to jiggle it a bit."

"Good to know," Jon said, accepting it and putting it immediately in a drawer by the door. Julie stood where she was for a moment, awkwardly, wanting to stay and talk but having no reason to.

"I guess Zelda and I should—"

"Uh, do you want a drink?" Jon interrupted. "A glass of wine? My nights off are the only time I can imbibe. I'm on my best behavior behind the bar."

Relieved, Julie nodded, accepting the offer. "I don't know if I could go five nights a week without wine. Good for you."

"Well, I am more of a beer kind of guy anyway."

"But, yeah, I'll take that glass," she said. "I guess it would be good for us to get to know each other a little better, now that we share Zelda."

Jon waved his arm at the reclining chairs. "Make yourself at home. Is pinot noir okay?"

"Perfect."

Jon slipped around her to get into the kitchen. Julie sat down on one of the La-Z-Boys and pushed back to lift the footrest. Zelda followed her and flopped down. Julie heard the cork pop and the friendly, welcome gurgle of wine. Jon walked back into the living room with a glass for her and a beer for himself.

"I was thinking, under this new arrangement, since we won't be walking together in the afternoon, maybe we could walk Zelda together on Sundays. Once in a while?" he said, lifting his glass for a clink with hers.

"Sure," Julie said. "That would be fun. To be honest, I don't have many friends here anymore. With college at UC-Davis, work at the store, and now a year in France, everyone sort of disappeared from my life."

Jon sat down in the other recliner and kicked his footrest up. "Same here. I came back after four years away and now I know no one. Only it was Iraq, not California and France."

Julie took a sip, letting the wine sit on her tongue for a moment. It was fine. Perhaps a French Burgundy, not an Oregon pinot, but fine just the same.

"Yeah, it turns out Cary's probably my best friend now. Imagine that. My little brother turns out to be my best friend."

Jon gestured toward her with his beer. "And right now, you and Zelda are mine."

A little embarrassed by his warmth, Julie hid her smile by leaning over and scratching Zelda's head. "She certainly seems comfortable here."

"I was worried at first that she'd smell Milo and there'd be a problem."

"Milo?"

"My dog. The one I got in Iraq," Jon said, his voice suddenly sad. "He was here for a couple of months."

Julie looked up. "Oh, right. I don't know how I forgot about Milo."

She took another sip and paused. "So, I have to ask: How did a guy who wants to be family lawyer end up in Iraq? They haven't reinstated the draft, have they?"

"No. No. It's a long story. Or, really the story's not so long. It just started a long time ago." He paused, as if uncertain he should continue.

"And ... ," Julie said to encourage him.

"Okay. If you really want to know." He took a long draw on his beer. "My dad was a lifer in the Marines. When I was just a kid he asked that I consider doing a stint in one of the services. He didn't make me promise I'd do it, but just that I'd think about it. So when I finished my undergraduate degree, I thought about it. And decided not to do it."

"But you did."

"Yeah. This is the hard part." He paused again, and Julie wondered if it was mean of her to insist on hearing the story.

Jon continued. "I was a semester through law school, and I got the news. Dad was hit by an IED in Afghanistan. Died right there."

"Oh, I'm so sorry. That's awful."

"Yeah. It was. Still is. But it made me reconsider. I signed up and ended up in Iraq. Stayed for four years."

"My god. I've never had to do anything so hard," she said.

"But what made it bearable was Milo," he said, his voice now wavering as if it were getting hard to hold back tears. "Milo got me through it."

Julie felt tears well up on her lids. "What kind of a dog was he?" she said, struggling to get the words out.

Jon pushed his footrest down and stood up to retrieve a photo album from his desk. He handed it to Julie.

Tentatively, she accepted it and let it fall open to the first photo. It was a picture of Milo with Jon in his fatigues in a desert setting, apparently Iraq. Milo looked like a shepherd of some sort—perhaps part German, perhaps Belgian. She looked through the pages of photos, unable to hold back the stream of tears they triggered. She closed the book, sniffling and wiping her eyes with the back of her hand.

Jon stood again and brought a box of Kleenex back to the end table and placed it between them.

"I'm sorry. I don't know why I'm … ." She couldn't finish the sentence. She gulped, grabbed a tissue, and blew her nose. She tried again. "He was beautiful."

Jon pulled a tissue and wiped his eyes.

"I'm really sorry," he said. "I didn't mean to upset you. I shouldn't have shown you that." He reached for the book.

Julie handed it back. "No, I'm glad you did. Like I said, we should get to know each other better. I understand so much more now. And now, I can see why you bonded with Zelda. And she with you."

Jon nodded, looking like he was struggling to talk. They looked away from each other and sipped their drinks.

After a couple of minutes, Julie broke the silence. "You know, this is kind of out of left field, but what do you think about going out to eat next week. On your night off?"

Jon laughed. "A date? I thought you were engaged."

Julie shook her head. "No, not a date. Of course not. But I'd like to take you out for dinner to thank you for taking such good care of Zelda for me. What do you think?"

Jon looked skeptical. "Does it have to be somewhere fancy?"

"Whatever you like. But I'd prefer not fancy."

Jon nodded in agreement. "How about Ivar's? Fish and chips?"

"I think I owe you more than fish and chips," Julie argued.

"You said whatever I like. I like fish and chips."

Julie laughed, the tension gone. "Okay. Okay. You'll get no argument from me. How about you meet me at the waterfront Ivar's at 7:15? On Wednesday. I'll text if I'm late."

Jon reached over and offered his hand. "Deal," he said. Julie accepted his gesture, and he held her hand longer than necessary.

Jon finally relinquished her fingers. "Too bad we can't bring Zelda."

Seven

Julie looked out across Puget Sound toward West Seattle from the picnic table outside of Ivar's and threw a couple of French fries as far as she could. Two gulls swept down, anticipating the spuds' flight and swooped them up just as they hit the water.

"You know, we're not supposed to feed the gulls. It only encourages them," said Jon, laughter in his voice.

"I know," said Julie. "But it's so much fun."

Jon shook his head and grinned broadly. "And you're a lot of fun, Julie." They smiled at each other over their paper bowls of fried fish and chips and dove back in.

"Thanks," she said, holding up a French fry as a toast.

Sitting side by side on the bench so they could both look out over the water, they munched for a few minutes, saying nothing. Julie wiped her greasy fingers on her napkin and reached for a fresh one. She loved fish and chips, but it was good that she didn't indulge in them too often.

"I'm sorry I gave you such a hard time when you came back," Jon said. "I was so afraid of losing Zelda."

Julie blinked in accord. "I understand. When I thought I'd lost her, it was the worst day of my life."

Jon tipped his head and looked out across the water with her. "Pretty easy life, huh?"

"I guess. So far," Julie said, recognizing the truth. She'd never lost a dog to cancer. Never gone into a battlefield. Never lost a father. "Not like yours."

"No. Not like mine," said Jon, soberly. "I've seen some pretty awful stuff." He paused. "Atrocities. Lost some good friends. Human ones. And of course, Milo." He pulled his eyes off the water and looked at Julie. "But I feel like I'm being rewarded now."

"How's that?" Julie stuffed a couple of fries in her mouth, ignoring the greedy, accusatory looks from the gulls sitting on the railing next to them.

"Well, getting to finish law school without debt. Getting to share Zelda. You."

Julie felt herself blush and looked away. "I know about your dad. Where is your mom?" she asked.

"She lives in Denver now. We don't talk much. After we lost Dad, she tried to talk me out of going to Iraq. She didn't want to lose me too. She hasn't forgiven me for scaring her like that."

Julie let that sink it. She did have it good, and she didn't mind Jon reminding her of that. Her parents were still together. They were entering retirement, well situated financially. She was set to inherit the wine store, a secure job already in place and a fiancé on his way across the Atlantic.

"I'm sorry. I am so lucky to still have my parents. They give me so much strength."

Jon bumped her on the shoulder. "I think you're pretty strong on your own."

"You're so nice to me, Jon," she said. "I don't think I've

ever dated a guy who was more thoughtful."

"But this isn't a date, remember?" he answered, teasing.

Julie looked down, embarrassed at her slip. "No, no. Of course not. I just meant all the guys I dated ... uh. I mean, of all the guys ... Oh, never mind."

She looked up at him bashfully. "Can I just ... kinda ... just slide out of this somehow?"

Jon laughed and threw his arm around her and pulled her to his side. "You do tend to get tangled up in your words sometimes."

Julie laughed with him. "Only around you. It only happens when I'm with you."

"Is that a good thing?"

"It's a thing. I'm not sure if it's good or bad."

Jon crumpled up his napkin and threw it in his empty paper bowl. "It's getting kind of deep here, don't you think? Maybe we should get back. Zelda needs her bedtime walk."

Julie wound her legs out from behind the seat and stood. They dumped their waste in a trash bin and Jon turned to her and swallowed her shoulders in a hug.

"Thanks for dinner, Julie. You sure know how to make a guy happy."

They stayed in the hug for a long moment before breaking apart and heading toward the bus stop.

At the neighborhood park the next Saturday, the week's drizzle continued, a little more robust than usual. Although the Seattle "wetness"—as residents called it—rarely required one, Jon and Julie shared an umbrella. Zelda walked ahead on a long leash, wrapped tightly in her raincoat.

Julie had the day off, as her mom and dad had decided to spend the day alone in the store, sort of a last-time, nostalgic tour of duty. It sounded almost romantic, Julie had said, and she was happy to give them the opportunity.

"I was thinking we should take Zelda out somewhere different sometime," Jon suggested. "Even dogs crave a change of scenery, don't you think? Maybe take her out to one of those dog beaches on the islands?"

"Yeah, maybe," Julie said. She'd been preoccupied all morning, and her tone was sullen.

"Oh, come on." Jon bumped against her. "I thought you'd like that." He watched her for a moment. "Is something wrong?"

"No," Julie said unconvincingly. She shrugged. "Well, yeah."

"Want to talk about it?"

"Not really." They walked a few more steps in silence. "Well, okay," she said. "I'm starting to wonder if André is really coming."

Jon didn't jump right in, and Julie wondered if he was considering whether that was good news or bad. Finally, he responded, "Why do you say that?"

"Well, he never calls me. When I text him, he doesn't text back. The only time we talk, I call him. And he's making no progress on getting here. It's the same story every time. Waiting for the chef to hire his replacement."

"Well, maybe it's just because it's a big move. Immigration isn't as easy as it used to be. Could be scary for a guy."

Julie nodded. They stopped to let Zelda pee and continued down the path.

"Yeah, I know," she said. She knew she sounded less than convinced.

"Give him some time," Jon added. "I'm sure he is still planning to come. It would be hard for any guy to stay away from you."

Julie smiled to herself. She wasn't the only one finding their relationship more than she had expected it to be. She turned toward him. "What? What did you say?"

Jon looked away. "I mean, you are engaged, right? It'd

be hard to turn your back on that, right?"

Julie laughed. She didn't want to embarrass him, even though she thought it was time for both of them to admit how close they had grown. She had a reason to hold back. Did he?

"Yeah. That's it," she said. "We are engaged. But thanks for the compliment."

Eight

Julie leafed through the pile of résumés that had come via email and in the mail at the store, trying to find one that impressed her. But nothing jumped out at her as saying, "I'm the one!" The amount of typos and misspellings was depressing enough. Adding to that was the fact that nearly all the applicants lacked any qualifications as a wine expert.

Her mother sat nearby, leafing through invoices and sorting them for payment.

"I have looked at so many résumés, the type is blurring," Julie whined.

Her mother looked up. "I don't know why you're having such a hard time finding the right person. The unemployment rate is so high. There's got to be lots of people looking for a retail job."

"Yeah, but I need someone who knows something about wine. Do you know every cover letter I've received from candidates talks about how much they love wine, but none of them have experience with anything but drinking it?"

"Well, maybe you'll just have to teach them," her mother said. "I had to teach you, you know."

Julie's eyes held fast on the résumé in front of her, but her mind wandered back to the after-school hours and Saturdays in the shop that had soaked up her teenage years. At first, all the wine descriptions and names of grape varieties just bounced off her as she wiped the dust from the shelves and bottles and listened to her mother's lectures. But by the time she was in high school, she had unconsciously absorbed much of it. She knew how the taste notes of an Oregon pinot noir differed from those in a French Burgundy, even though the grape was supposedly the same; she knew that Beaujolais was made with the gamay grape; and the Sancerre from the Loire was not only acidic but was forever linked to the French resistance in World War II. Her friends were out riding their bikes down the steep alleys of First Hill and hanging out in the market, smoking cigarettes with the cool art school students. But she was perfectly happy to be flying over the high, dry mesas of the Rioja region in her imagination, as her father described his travels in Franco's Spain, dodging fascist spies who trailed him through vineyards and villages as if he knew anything that might be of interest to them.

She shook herself out of her reverie.

"Yes, I learned it all, but it took years," she said. "And the easy part of this job is holding down the sales floor—showing wine, helping people choose a bottle for dinner and for a party. But that can't be learned overnight, and I need to be back in the office, doing the hard stuff. The books, the ordering, the marketing, the website, the shipping … ."

Her mother laughed. She had been in a better mood

lately, now that her retirement was fast approaching. "You're making the job I did all my life sound awful, Julie. I liked it."

"No. I don't mean to. I just mean we need someone up front who knows what they're talking about."

"Keep looking. That person is out there."

Julie hoped her mother was right. She had no idea how she was going to take care of the store all by herself in two weeks when her mom and dad took off.

"What do you hear from André?" her mother asked, standing up to pour herself another cup of coffee.

Julie sighed and leaned forward on the counter, her head in her hands.

"Same old. Same story. Still waiting for the chef to replace him."

"You think there's a problem?"

"I don't know," Julie said, her thoughts suddenly across the ocean with André. "I just don't know. And the problem is, there's no one who can help me figure it out. Jon thinks there's nothing to worry about, but I don't know."

"Didn't you still have some friends over there who knew him? Can't you ask someone in Paris?"

"My mentor at the restaurant knows him. He introduced us. But if I call him, he'll tell André, and I don't want to make a big deal out of this." She paused and tried to pull her focus back to the résumés. "Maybe there is no problem, and I'll just spook André if he thinks I'm checking up on him."

Julie looked at her mom and shrugged. Her mother smiled reassuringly. "I understand. Maybe just give him a little more time. You've got plenty to do here."

The front door chimes rang, and they looked up to see Cary walking in. He stopped at a new end-cap display Julie had just constructed to feature wines of Washington's Columbia Gorge.

"What are you doing here?" their mother asked.

Cary looked up at her, a bit of sneer on his face. It was a look Julie knew usually meant he had something to hide or something he needed to confess that he'd prefer to keep a secret.

"What? Can't I stop by?" He sounded just as defensive as Julie had expected. "You were happy to see me when you needed me. Before your darling Julie got back."

Julie and her mother exchanged knowing glances.

"No, I mean, don't you have to work today?"

"No. Not today," Cary said.

"Did you quit? Again?"

Julie stayed out of the exchange. Her mother was a bit harder on Cary than Julie liked, but she had to admit that Cary deserved much of the criticism he got.

"Not exactly," Cary said, walking away from her, down one of the aisles, picking up a bottle here and there, stalling.

"Then, what, exactly?"

"Got fired."

Her mother snickered. "Well, color me surprised. What did you do?"

Cary looked at Julie. Did he expect her to intervene? She had a number of times over their lifetime in their parents' house, but it had never done much to soften her mother's disappointment in her son. Julie shook her head. She couldn't help.

"It doesn't matter," Cary said. He replaced the bottle he'd been studying and shoved his hands in his jeans pockets. "It was time for me to go. I couldn't do it much longer. It was like a prison. Pay was good. Benefits great. But I couldn't stand the clock, the ticking clock. The supervisors. The quotas. It just wasn't right for me."

Julie's mother shook her head. "Well, Cary, life can't be a wine tasting party all the time. You're going to have to find something that's right for you pretty soon."

"I know. I just thought I should come and tell you before you found out from someone else."

He waved at Julie. "Hey, sis," he said. "How's Zelda? And Jon?"

"Fine," Julie said, happy to help him change the subject. "We're going to the dog beach on Sunday. Want to come along?"

"Nah." Cary shook his head. "I'm playing golf with Ted."

He turned back to their mother. "Tell Dad about the job for me, will you? I don't think I can face him right now."

He exaggerated a sigh. Cary continued down the aisle and out the door without another word.

"Can't either of my kids ever be happy?" Mother asked, shaking her head at Julie.

"I'm not so sure Cary isn't happy," Julie answered. "He's just lost for the moment."

"Well, it's been one very long moment."

Nine

THE MORNING THAT JON AND Julie drove to the ferry terminal, rode the Tokitae across to Whidbey Island, and followed the meandering, narrow roads to the leash-free Double Bluff Beach, it was low tide, and the dark sand stretched 300 yards from the bluff to the foamy water of Puget Sound.

The chilly breeze off the water didn't faze Zelda. She darted straight for the edge of the water with abandon and high-stepped through the surf, grinning like only dog owners know a dog can. Julie pulled her down jacket tight around her chest and shivered.

"Let's walk," she said. "Zelda won't let us out of her sight. As much as she may dream of running away when she's on a leash, she's really a mommy's girl."

"You think so?" Jon's voice was teasing. "Maybe she's really a daddy's girl."

Julie laughed. "I suppose she could be both."

They walked along the hard-packed sand near the water and watched Zelda stop and sniff, run ahead, turn around to sniff something she just about missed, and then leap ahead again. The girl was having a blast and suddenly Julie felt guilty for not taking her to the beach more often. There was a dog beach in Seattle too, along the west side of Lake Washington, but it was always crowded, and as gregarious as Zelda was with people, she tended to be shy around dogs she didn't know. Whenever Julie took her there, Zelda hung around the picnic table where Julie sat, often hiding under her knees. She didn't look like she was having a good time.

Zelda stopped ahead and looked straight out across the water.

"Perhaps she can see Russia from there," Jon joked. "Do you think she's thinking of swimming there?"

"Not Russia. But maybe Vancouver. After I adopted her from the rescue agency, I always thought she might be part Canadian," Julie said.

"Why?"

They fell into an easy pace that suited both Julie's long strides and Jon's long legs.

"I was taking French lessons before I went to France," Julie answered, "and she seemed to understand French better than English."

"Hmmm." Jon nodded. "I think they respond to your tone of voice. You were probably being more expressive in French. You know, trying to learn intonation."

Julie wondered why she hadn't thought of that. She knew how faithfully Zelda responded to different pitches of her voice.

"It scares me how smart you are," Julie said.

"That's odd coming from you. I have thought you might be much smarter than me. What was your degree in?"

Julie felt herself blush at the compliment, the heat in her cheeks welcome, even as she hoped Jon wouldn't look over to notice. "Double major. French literature and viticulture. And yours?"

"Interesting combination. Renaissance-like. Mine was history, of course."

"Ah, yes," Julie said. "Makes sense as a pre-law degree, right?"

Their conversation shifted from family and schools to old friends and former pets as they continued down the beach, following Zelda. They bumped into each other every few steps, the lumpy sand making walking a perfectly straight line difficult.

Zelda stopped to sniff something at the water's edge in front of them. "Don't you dare roll in that!" Julie yelled into the breeze, as she watched. With her eyes on Zelda, she tripped on a piece of driftwood, and Jon caught her by the elbow. He slipped her arm under his and pulled it in close.

Julie's heart skipped. What did this mean? Was this simply a kind gesture by Jon to make sure she didn't fall or was there more meaning to it than that? She waited for her heartbeat to return to normal and decided she wouldn't read too much into it. It felt good, whatever his intention.

Despite the brisk breeze, Julie started to warm up. Was it the walk or the proximity to Zelda's new dad? She wasn't sure, but she slowly realized she was smiling. Broadly. Unabashedly. It had been a while since she had felt this kind of unforced happiness. She had been happy with André too, but it had always been something she had felt separate from—outside of, actually—imagining how other women would see her and consider her lucky, or how someday she'd look back at her time with him in Paris with nostalgia.

"Hey, a perfect bench," Jon said, pointing to a large log sitting parallel to the water and Zelda's trajectory. "Think if we sit, Zelda will hang close?"

"Sure," Julie said. "She's not going far whether she's a mommy's girl or a daddy's girl."

Julie picked out a flat spot on the wood and sat, glad she'd worn a pair of old jeans that wouldn't show a little salt or sap stain. Jon sat next to her, close enough that he could pull her arm back through his again. They sat, watching Zelda play in the wet sand, entertaining herself like the only child she was.

"She's going to be a mess after this," Julie said, shaking her head to get her wind-blown hair out of her face. "I think she should go home with you."

"Ha!" Jon laughed. "Nope. I just vacuumed, remember?"

"That was a week ago Wednesday! You mean you haven't vacuumed since then?"

"Okay, when was the last time you did?"

Julie faked a sniff. "I have an excuse. I'm trying to keep the store running, find an assistant and plan a retirement party for my parents."

Jon looked over and pushed a wind-blown lock of her long bangs out of her eyes. It was an intimate gesture, one that Julie couldn't ignore as easily as she had dismissed the way he held her arm.

"When's the party?" Jon asked.

Julie fought to keep her voice calm as heat rose again to her face. "Just a few days. It's a Wednesday night, so I was hoping you could come and bring Zelda by. Lots of our customers know her."

"Sure," Jon said, still looking intently at her face. His voice sounded cool, not sexy or romantic, but his body language was communicating something else. "Sounds like fun. She won't knock the bottles off the shelves with her tail?"

"It'll be your job to make sure she doesn't," Julie said. "And she's really good in the shop, even with all those bottles." Her words were neutral and platonic, but she realized how much she had lowered her voice. Was she flirting?

They sat in silence for a few minutes, Julie relieved that

Jon's focus had returned to Zelda's antics. Her blush faded, and she concentrated on breathing slowly and deeply. Finally, feeling like she had regained control of her voice again, she spoke.

"I think this thing is really working out for Zelda." She paused, uncertain if she should continue. "And for us. What do you think?"

Jon turned to her and held her eyes. "It's working out very well for me," he said, his voice low now too. He leaned closer and looked down at her lips. For a moment, neither of them did anything. Then he slipped his hand behind her neck, and Julie closed her eyes, waiting for his kiss. Had she known this was going to happen? How long had she known?

Whoosh!

Just before their lips touched, eighty pounds of wet, sandy dog plowed into them, dumping them backwards onto the beach.

"Zelda!" they yelled in unison, arms and legs flying as they fell. They pulled themselves up on their elbows and laughed.

Julie struggled to her knees and stood up, brushing as much wet sand as she could off her clothes and out of her hair. Jon still lay on the ground with Zelda prancing around him, barking as if she'd discovered a new game. Jon was laughing too hard to get up. Julie reached down and offered him a hand. He pulled upright, and she started to work on the crusty sand that covered his backside.

"Well, that was a shocker," Julie said.

"You think she knew what we were about to do?" Jon asked. He stopped and looked at Julie, a different question in his eyes.

"I'm not sure I did," Julie said. She shook her head and looked away. "Do you mind if we … ? I really need to forget that just about happened. I'm en—," she started to say, but she couldn't get the word out.

"Yes, I know you're engaged. I'm sorry." Jon looked as remorseful as he sounded. He took her hands and met her eyes, an apology written on his face.

"Do you mind?" she repeated, afraid he'd try to kiss her again.

Jon paused for a moment, holding her hands between then, before letting go with a sad shrug.

"No," he said. He pulled Zelda's leash out of his coat pocket. "I think it's time we headed back."

Ten

Retirement parties were never Julie's thing. She had to attend dozens of them with her parents over the past few years, as their friends had all reached their own magic number—55 or 60 or 65—the age at which they had promised themselves they would hang up the spurs and walk hand in hand into the sunset.

As generous as she tried to be with her time, sympathies, and kindliness, the parties always left her drained of every ounce of congeniality and impossible to be around for the following days.

This one had to be different. It was for her own parents. It was their swan song. She owed them so much for providing her with a career, a job, a business—all things that her classmates and friends had to struggle and beg for from unrelated, disinterested employers and bankers. It was all so easy for her.

Easy, if she didn't consider the after-school hours and

weekends she was committed to working for Mom and Dad from the time she was about fourteen. Yes, she had it made now, but she'd given up a lot of what it meant to be a kid to earn it.

Was that why Julie had such a soft spot for Cary? Why she didn't write him off the way her parents seemed inclined to? She recognized he was, in many ways, more normal than she was. It was normal to search for an identity, to rebel, to struggle to figure out what you wanted to do "when you grew up." If Cary had problems keeping a job, if he jumped from one thing to another, it was only because he hadn't yet matched a profession or a position to his personality. It would come to him, Julie was convinced. He was smart, good-hearted, and gregarious. And he was still young. Plenty of time, she told her parents. "Quit riding him."

As she slipped around and between the well-wishers who had shown up at the "Going Sailing" party she was throwing for her parents, Julie realized how many of their faces she recognized and names she knew. Would it be the same in forty years when it came time for her to get on the sailboat—or the jet plane or the highway—and disappear into happy retirement? Would she have regular customers, friends and neighbors among the shops up and down their street? Or would retail stores be a thing of the past, replaced by fast, overnight delivery and online wine stores that wouldn't require customers to leave their houses and find a parking spot just to get a bottle of bubbly for an anniversary dinner at home?

Maybe her future wasn't so certain after all.

Setting a tray of cheese and charcuterie on the table where Cary was serving wine, she waited for him to finish what he was doing.

"Let me know what you think of this mourvèdre," he was saying to Christine Mayer, one of the shopkeepers in the neighborhood who had retired in the past year.

"Thanks, I will," Christine said, winking at Cary. Julie smiled. Her brother was handsome, and even if he was as worthless as her mother thought, the women at the party seemed to approve of him. Even those twice his age.

"You're getting really good at this, Cary," she said as Christine rejoined her husband in a small knot of friends. "Maybe you should look into getting a job in a wine-tasting room in the Columbia Valley."

Cary rewarded her compliment with a quick frown. "I don't know anyone there," he said curtly.

"Didn't you meet some of the distributors when you were covering for me here last year?"

"Yes, distributors. But their wine tastings are in supermarkets. I can't think of anything worse than standing all day in a supermarket."

Julie pulled the plastic wrap off the tray she was delivering and adjusted its placement. She accepted an empty tray from Cary. "What's wrong with supermarkets?"

Cary shrugged and avoided her eye. What was his problem today? Usually they got along wonderfully. "They're sterile, I guess."

"Well, once I get done with this party, I'll make a few calls for you. I know marketing people in the Tri-Cities."

"Well, don't you worry about me," he snarled.

"Hey, what's wrong?" Julie asked. "Did I say something?"

"Never mind." He dismissed her and smiled up at a tall man who had just approached the table with an empty glass. "What can I get for you? The same or do you want to try something different?"

Julie shook her head and walked away. She stopped next to her mother, who was momentarily standing alone, watching the partygoers mingle.

"What's wrong with Cary?" Julie asked.

Her mother looked surprised. "Nothing, as far as I know. He really likes these wine-tastings. And he's good at it. He knows his wine. He helped us a lot this past year when you were gone."

Julie watched Cary interact with a couple more guests before she headed back to the office to refill the tray.

Just as she let the door close behind her, she heard her mother shout. "Zelda! Come here sweetie!"

Julie put the empty tray down and opened the door to watch Zelda run toward her mother, Jon trailing behind her, holding her leash. Her mother leaned down to give the shaggy dog a hug and accepted a quick lick on the face from Zelda's big tongue. Julie let the door swing closed again and stood with her ear close, listening.

"You must be Jon," her mom said. "I'm Ellie, Julie's mom. She's told us all about you. You're an angel for helping her take care of Zelda."

"Well, it's my pleasure. I think of Zelda as mine, too. Fifty percent responsible for her."

"That's great. Here, let me take her for a minute," Julie's mom said. "She needs to say hi to some old friends of ours. You go get a glass of wine."

"Is Julie here?" Jon asked.

"Sure. She just went into the back."

Julie scrambled away from the door and got busy arranging another tray of cheeses and meats. When Jon walked in, she looked up, pretending to be surprised.

"Hey." She tried to sound calm, but her mind's eye kept seeing their near kiss on the beach a few days before. She wasn't sure how Jon was going to treat her now. She'd kept her distance the past four days, letting Jon come and go to retrieve and return Zelda, making sure she wouldn't be there when he did.

"Yeah, hey," Jon responded. He stood by the door, his hands in his jeans pockets.

"Did you bring Zelda?" It was disingenuous. Julie knew the answer, but it seemed like the safest topic.

"Yes, your mother took her from me. Seems everyone loves Zelda."

"So you met my mom."

"Yeah. She said you'd told her a lot about me."

"Well, Cary and I both." Julie blushed. "Some. Don't get a big head about it." She continued unwrapping tubes of sausage and arranging the slices on the tray. She didn't look, but she could sense Jon fidgeting.

"What is it?" she asked. "Something bothering you?"

"I think we should talk about what happened on the beach on Sunday," he said quietly. Exactly what she was afraid he'd say.

"I know you are engaged," he continued. "And I know you are still expecting André to come. But I'd like to know about us. Do you think there something here? Do you have any feelings for me?"

Julie was surprised he spoke so bluntly. She would have beat around the bush, if it had been her desire to talk about it. She put the sausage down and wiped her hands on her apron. She turned to him soberly.

"Jon," she said. "I'm sorry. It was just the beach. Walking Zelda. The fresh air. The surf. Whatever. I didn't think anything about it. You shouldn't think anything about it, either."

Jon shuffled his feet and looked away. Julie started to load wine glasses on another tray, wiping them off with a cloth, setting them upside down on a layer of napkins.

"It was just the moment, huh? Nothing else?"

Julie looked up. "You said it yourself. I'm engaged. I'm not going to obsess about what almost happened but didn't." She picked up the tray and handed it to him. The glasses rattled against each other, betraying her shaking hands.

"Here. Can you take those out to Cary for me?"

Jon nodded sadly and turned to the door. He pushed it open with a hip and slipped through with the tray, like a professional waiter. André couldn't have done it better.

Julie watched him go before turning around and burying her face in her hands. She took a deep breath.

"André," she whispered. "Get your butt over here soon. Before I do something stupid."

The crowd had thinned to just a handful of couples by the time the party reached its advertised duration. No one was pushing the stragglers out the door. If her parents' best friends hung out for another hour, that was fine.

Jon had left just fifteen minutes after he dropped off Zelda, and Cary had disappeared. Zelda was zonked out on her doggie bed, and Julie was mellowing out with a glass of a fine Rhone wine she wouldn't have bought for herself. Up until Saturday, July 1, the store profit and loss was her parents' problem, not hers.

A half hour later, the crowd was gone, and Julie and her mother gathered up unused napkins and paper plates, and tossed out the used ones.

"I liked Jon a lot," her mother said. "So did your father. Is there anything going on there, Jules? Between the two of you?"

Julie rolled her eyes. "Mom. I'm engaged." She looked away, worried her eyes would then betray her. "There is nothing going on with Jon except Zelda."

"Well, I saw the way he looked at you. There's something there, dear, at least for him. Are you sure you don't like him?"

Julie sighed loudly. "Of course, I like him. He's smart and ambitious and he loves Zelda. What's not to like?"

"And yet, you're still waiting on André. This mysterious André." Julie wasn't sure, but it sounded like her mother clucked her tongue.

She stopped working and threw her hands on her hips. "Mother. André is not mysterious. I'm sure he's coming any day now."

"Has he said so?"

Julie gestured at the remains of the party fixings. "In case you haven't noticed, I've been a bit busy here over the past couple of weeks." She changed the subject. "By the way, what happened to Cary?"

"He left a half hour ago. Seemed in one of his moods. I thanked him for taking care of the bar."

"I talked to him about finding a job in the wine industry," Julie said. "Maybe over in the Tri-Cities or Walla Walla."

"And what did he say?"

Julie shook her head. "He kind of blew me off. He said he doesn't know anyone there. But I'll make a few calls next week. See if anything is available. He's a good-looking guy. Personable … most of the time."

Julie's father walked around the end of the aisle and put his arm over Julie's shoulder. He kissed her on the forehead. "Jules, you put on quite the soirée." He put his other arm around her mother's shoulder and pulled her close. "We can't thank you enough."

"You can thank me by finding me an assistant before you leave. You guys are still hoping to leave end of next week, right?"

Her father nodded. He understood the situation. "Maybe Cary can help out until you find someone. He did some of that when you were in France."

"But, can I depend on him?" Julie asked. "You know I love him, but he doesn't do reliable very well."

"Yes, you're right," her father said. "Well, it was just a thought." He picked up an empty charcuterie plate and a plastic tub of dirty wine glasses. "I'll take these back for you."

Eleven

THE NEXT DAY, JULIE WALKED into her apartment after work, and was greeted excitedly—as usual—by Zelda. She put her purse down on the table, and saw a note, a small bag of doggie treats, and a small box of Seattle chocolates.

She picked up the note and opened it.

> I thought you and Zelda needed some Treats. Thanks for inviting me to the party the other night. Your parents are cool. XO Jon PS: Sorry about obsessing over the other day. I'm over it.

"Hmmm," Julie murmured. "I hope I can get over it too."

She opened the bag of dog treats.

"Sit!" she ordered Zelda, who complied as she always did. "That's from your buddy, Jon."

Julie had called him "daddy" at the beach the other day, but after their near-kiss, that seemed too dangerous.

She opened the little box of chocolates, chose one, walked over to the chair by the window, sat and looked out, nibbling on the chocolate. When she finished, she reached for her phone and texted:

Thanks for the chocolates and the treats. If not for Andre maybe things would be different.

That was as close as she wanted to come to admitting the truth. She stopped to think and then backspaced over the second sentence before hitting "send."

IT WAS ONLY EIGHT DAYS before her parents planned to leave "forever"—at least until winter weather on the west coast of Canada and Alaska made sailing treacherous—and Julie was still looking for an assistant. Late morning, she stood behind the counter at the store, looking over three piles of résumés: "definitely not," "maybe," and the shortest pile, "call."

She wasn't eager to start making those calls, knowing how hard it was to get much of a feel for people over the phone. Instead, she picked up her phone and dialed. Jon answered quickly.

"Hey," she said. "I wondered if you can drop Zelda off here on your way to work. I'm going to be working really late tonight."

"Sure," he said. All the awkwardness between them seemed to have dissipated, to Julie's relief. "Is something wrong there?"

"No, nothing's wrong. I'm just trying to get through these calls to assistant candidates. And I had to let Mom off the hook tonight. She needs to finish packing for their big adventure."

"Right," Jon said. "I'll be there about five."

Julie hung up but she stood for a few minutes, staring out the window, distracted by her thoughts.

A few hours later, Julie had lined up three in-person interviews with candidates from her "call" pile. She stood in the French Burgundy section, listening as a customer described her recent Backroads bike tour of the region.

"And the food," the woman said, dramatically clasping her stomach with both hands. "The food! It was incredible."

"Yes, it is hard to miss with those wine tours," Julie responded, patiently. She knew the type—the customers who wanted to talk and impress, and only rarely bought. They wanted exactly the same wine they'd had that night on the Loire, when … blah, blah, blah, but the wineries visited by the American-run tours weren't usually the ones that exported wine to the U.S. Even less likely were they to distribute on America's West Coast. "And so what are you thinking you'd like to try today? Making dinner tonight?"

The customer shifted her big shopping tote on her shoulder and picked up a random bottle, turning it over to look at the tasting notes. "I'm not sure," she mumbled. "Maybe I'll see something that trips my trigger."

"I'll be happy to help if you have any questions," Julie said, retreating back to the counter to wait. This customer, she knew, would be "just looking" for a couple more minutes to ensure that Julie thought she had been worth her time, and then she'd slip out the door.

As she sat back down on her stool behind the counter, Julie's cellphone buzzed. She looked at the incoming text:

WHAT'S YOUR PARENTS NUMBER?

Oh, André! It had been four days since she'd heard from him. He always used all caps, as if he were Donald

Trump. But why was he asking for the address? Did he plan to ship them some wine?

She typed in the address, adding "Why?"

She waited. No answer.

The customer slipped out, setting off the door chime, and Julie called out, "Thanks for coming by. Let me know if I can ever help you find something." She returned to her phone screen, waiting for André's response. The door chime rang again. Julie looked up and nearly dropped her phone.

"André! Is it really you?"

Her dark, handsome fiancé was walking toward her, his arms outstretched and a huge smile on his face. Julie ran out from behind the counter into his arms and let him envelop her in a long, tight hug. She pulled back and tipped her head up for his kiss.

"So this is why you needed the address," she said. She pretended to pout. "And here I thought you were sending us some great French vintage."

"Oh, disappointed, are you?" he said, laughing. "Maybe I should go back and—" she interrupted him, locking her lips on his again. It felt like she was back in Paris, her heart pounding, her love soaring.

Finally, they separated, and André followed her back to the stools behind the counter. "Sorry I didn't call," he explained. "I only thought to text for the exact address when I was in the neighborhood."

"Oh, no need to apologize!" she assured him. "But such a surprise? Why no warning?" She leaned forward toward him and put her hands on his knees.

"I'm sorry, I didn't think you needed one. Chef found someone and he let me go right away. So here am I!" André got up and sauntered down one of the aisles of wine stacks. "So, this is the shop I heard so much about."

Julie watched him walk slowly down a row of Washington wines, pick up a bottle here and there, and study the labels. "Do Americans always list the varietals on their labels?" he asked.

"Not always. Not usually with typical Bordeaux blends, but often with the Rhones, sometimes with the Spanish and Italian varietals," she said. As she watched him move around the store, she was struck by how he was dressed. He looked so French, something she'd first noticed in Paris but had forgotten. He wore skin-tight jeans and a silk scarf, a tight-fitting sweater and low leather boots. The gay men of Seattle would pick him out of a crowd in an instant, she thought.

Finally, he'd exhausted his interest in the wine and returned to her side. "*Puis, comment ça va?* When are you going to start being the boss? Have your parents traveled?"

"No, they're leaving this weekend for Alaska. I'm still trying to find an assistant. So I'm afraid the next few weeks are going to be kind of hectic."

André scooted close and parted her knees. He slipped his legs between hers and held her head with both hands. He pulled her eyes close to his. "You are making an excuse to not see me?" he whispered.

Julie felt a crooked smile cross her face. Maybe she was. But why? In the ten minutes André had been in the shop, her initial elation at seeing him had dulled. Was it now a mild revulsion?

What was so French about him thrilled her in Paris. Now she wondered if he could ever seem at home in Seattle.

"Hey, I know! While you're looking for a job, you could come and help me out," she said to cover her ambivalence.

André shook his head. "I don't think I can do that. I don't know about wine."

"It won't matter. People will hear you talk. and they'll think, 'Ah, he's French. He must know his wine.'"

André laughed and leaned in to peck her on the lips.

"Let's close up the shop and go celebrate," he said. "I can't believe I'm finally here with you."

Julie slipped off the stool and shuffled the résumés. She didn't want to brush him off, but she was confused. Why had she so quickly lost her enthusiasm for this man she'd waited so long to see?

"Hey, *cherie*," André said. "What's wrong? Not glad to see me?"

Julie fought the urge to say yes. "Oh, no, André. I'm thrilled that you're here. It's just that I have a lot to do tonight. I have three interviews with possible assistants tomorrow."

André moved in behind her and wrapped his arms around her from the back. Just then, the door chime rang, and Julie turned to see Jon walking in with Zelda, his focus on keeping the leash from tangling in the door. Julie caught her breath, and Jon looked up.

"Oh!" he exclaimed. He looked startled and deflated at the same time. There was no chance he didn't know who this man standing behind her was. He looked the part. He was acting the part.

Julie shook herself loose from André's arms and darted around the counter to take Zelda's leash.

"Uh, J-J-Jon," she said, nearly tripping over his name. Was she embarrassed at being discovered in her fiancé's arms? She gestured at André. "This is André. André, this is Jon. Jon and I are sharing custody of Zelda."

Julie leaned down and let her hand roll down Zelda's back as he headed back behind the counter toward André.

Jon forced a smile and nodded toward André, extending his hand over the counter. "Nice to meet you, André. I've heard much about you."

André ignored the hand, looking sideways at Jon. "*Ami o frere?*" he asked.

"Uh, Jon doesn't speak French, André," Julie interjected.

"*Ami,*" Jon answered. "*Buen ami.*"

"Oh! *Excusez moi!*" Julie laughed nervously. "I didn't know."

She stood back and looked back and forth between them. Her eyes stuck on Jon's and she gave him an embarrassed shrug.

"We met because of Zelda," Jon said with not a bit of uncertainty. "I'm sure Julie will tell you all about it." He saluted Julie and backed down the aisle. "But I have to get to work. Welcome to the U.S., André. I hope you like it here."

Jon turned and left quickly, and Zelda whined after him. André watched him leave, narrowed his eyes just for a second, as if understanding something, and turned to smile at Julie.

"He seems nice. And you two...?"

Julie picked up the résumés again and tapped them against the counter to straighten the pile.

"Oh, nothing. No. I didn't even know he spoke French. He kept Zelda while I was in France, and now we share her so we can both work."

André seemed to accept that without concern. "Oh, and where does Jon work?"

"He's a bartender at a restaurant downtown. A very nice restaurant."

"Maybe he can put in a word for me with the chef," André said.

"I'll ask him, but he doesn't do much with the kitchen."

Zelda leaned against Julie's leg, begging for some attention. Julie leaned down and hugged her as André watched. Clearly, he wasn't charmed.

"I should get myself settled, and you should get your work done so we can start spending our time together," he said, giving Zelda and Julie wide berth as he headed toward the door.

"Where are you staying?"

"I've lodged myself at the Kimpton. Is it nice?"

"Yes." Julie nodded. "I think you'll be comfortable there. It has a kind of Euro vibe. I'd come by tonight. but you probably need some sleep. Jet lag and all. And I need to take Zelda home. So, how about I call you tomorrow and we'll see …" She stopped. What questions could there be?

André's eyes reflected her confusion. "See what?"

Julie scrambled to explain. "Uh, see how we can help find you a job," she ad-libbed.

André stepped toward her again and put his hands on her hips. He raised her face to his with a finger.

"I am very happy to see you, Julie." He leaned in for a kiss, and Julie let him brush his lips against hers, her eyes open, looking across the room and out the door.

Twelve

Out on Zelda's morning walk the next day, Julie pulled her cellphone from her pocket and called André's cellphone. His answering service declared his voice mailbox full. She looked the number up for the Kimpton, stored it in her contacts, and dialed it.

The receptionist transferred her call to André's room. An answering machine demanded in a smarmy monotone, "Leave a message for … [André's voice] André Lebover … then hang up or press pound for more options."

Julie waited for the beep.

"Hi, André. I hope you slept well," she dictated. "Why don't you come by the shop today about noon. I'll order out for sandwiches. Okay? Okay. *Bientot*."

She hung up and dropped the phone back into her coat pocket.

"Oh, what are we going to do, Zelda? What are we going to do?"

Zelda looked up at her, and Julie was struck again, like she had been hundreds of times, how clearly the dog understood exactly what she meant. The dog shook a bit of water off her raincoat and plodded forward through the puddles as if to say, "All we can do, Mom, is keep moving."

"That's right," Julie answered. "We'll just shake it off. Get back with the program." They splashed through another dozen steps. "André it is."

At noon, she and André were eating cream cheese and prosciutto sandwiches at the counter in the store, and Julie had started to feel less conflicted about his presence. Perhaps her earlier anxiety had more to do with worries about the store than concern about her relationship with her fiancé. And it looked like everything was working out.

"I think I may have found an assistant," she said. "I interviewed someone this morning who seems like she's great for the job. She obviously knows her wine and she's worked in retail."

"Great. Then you won't be so busy." André looked pleased. He reached over and put his hand on hers. "You can pay more attention to me, now that I'm here. I will not be alone."

Yes, Julie thought, suddenly feeling like her sanguinity had taken a step backward. Of course, he would think only in terms of what this meant for him.

"What do you mean?" she asked, forcing herself to stay pleasant when she really wanted to ask, "Why is everything always about you?"

"You don't feel the same here, Julie. You seem distant."

Again, she chose not to argue. "It's work. It's just tough now until I get some help. I'll be fine. Really I will."

André, however, must have caught something in her tone. He pushed his dark eyebrows so close together they almost touched in the middle, above his long, Latin nose.

"You still want to get married ... ?" He lifted her chin with a finger, forcing her to look into his eyes. It wasn't a question and it wasn't a statement. Something in between.

"Of course," Julie answered quickly, shaking her head loose. "Of course. Once you get a job and get settled, we can talk about it."

"Just talk? Or actually get married?"

"Plan," she said. "Yes, plan to get married."

André's eyebrows relaxed and he smiled broadly. "Good. I know how you Americans go for your big weddings. I'm looking forward to seeing ours!"

Julie couldn't help smiling back. His grin had always cheered her, even on dreary days in Paris, when she'd wondered if she'd ever get back home.

"Yes, me too," she said, mainly to close the topic. It wasn't necessarily true. She couldn't imagine summoning up the excitement to plan one of those multi-thousand-dollar weddings that some of her old classmates had staged in the past few years. She wasn't close to any of these women anymore, but she guessed they got some return on their investment, if only more stuff from their Amazon.com gift registration.

"Hey, do you think you could talk to Jon about his restaurant?" André asked. "Maybe they need a chef? Or maybe he knows some other kitchens, can ask around?"

Julie hated this topic too. She didn't feel like asking Jon to help André find a job, given the way she knew Jon felt about him. Or really, about her with him. But she couldn't admit that to André.

"Sure, I'll ask him. He isn't too involved with the restaurant scene. He's actually in law school. Doesn't have much time to socialize."

"Law school?" André jerked his head toward her, surprised. "He's going to be an attorney? I thought he was a bartender. A barrister? That's impressive."

Julie laughed. "Well, attorneys … not so much in the U.S. There are already too many lawyers."

Her phone buzzed, and she picked it up off the counter and checked the caller ID.

"Hi, Jon," she said in the most neutral voice she could manage.

"Hey, Julie," he said. "Hey, I hate to ask, knowing you are probably busy now with André, but could you keep Zelda this weekend? I mean, no back and forth?"

"Oh," she said. "Something come up?"

"Yeah," he said. He sounded like he was trying to be cheerful, not like he really was. "I have to go out of town. I'll be back in time for online classes on Monday. I can watch her as usual during the day."

"Okay, sure. That's fine," she said. "Zelda and I can find something to do on our own this weekend. No problem."

Jon lowered his voice. "Is André there? I mean, with you now?"

"Yes, he's here." Julie looked up and nodded at her fiancé. André bumped her elbow and held up a finger.

"Just a moment," she said into the phone, and covered the speaker.

"*Qué?*" she asked.

André whispered, "Ask him about jobs. About the kitchen. Maybe he can ask the chef to talk to me."

Julie fought the urge to roll her eyes but nodded and turned back to the phone.

"Sorry. I'm back."

"What was that about?"

"Well, he wants to know if you can introduce him to the chef there."

"Uh … ." Jon paused. "I really don't think so. It's not my place to … ." He stopped. Julie looked up at André's anxious face.

"Okay. Sure," she said, as if he'd really had an answer for

her. "Well, have a nice trip. Zelda will miss you."

Julie hung up and André grabbed her arm. "What did he say?"

"He said he'd ask." Julie put down the phone and looked away, hiding what probably looked like a guilty face.

"Maybe I should talk to Jon. Tell him my credentials."

"Sure, but that will have to wait. He called to tell me he's going out of town for the weekend. We usually walk Zelda together on Sundays. He had to let me know he can't do it this weekend."

André leaned back and knit his eyebrows again. "You are close, *n'est-ce pas*? Closer than you tell me?"

"No," Julie said. She shook her head. "It's just Zelda. We only spend time together with Zelda."

"Okay. I will walk with you and Zelda Sunday. Where do we go?"

"Yes. That's good. You can meet me in the morning tomorrow too, if you want to walk. We get out about six."

"It is not dark?"

Julie stood up and started to gather up their sandwich wrappers and napkins. "This is Seattle. It's light by 4:30."

André looked shocked, and Julie laughed. "Didn't you see that this morning?"

"Uh, *non*. I was sleeping until 10."

"So, *oui ou non*? You coming?"

Thirteen

If André wanted to reignite Julie's romantic feelings toward him, joining her and Zelda on a morning walk didn't accomplish it.

They stepped into the park in what Julie thought was a pleasant mist. Having lived in Seattle all of her life except for the fourteen months in Paris, she considered a misty day "wet" but not "rainy." Rainy was rare in Seattle, but from September through June "wet" was kind of usual. It felt nice, cool even. Sweet on the skin. Better than the harsh sun she experienced on a vacation trip to Palm Springs one winter.

"Do you have an umbrella?" André asked.

Julie looked askance. "For this?" she asked, holding out her hand to show how little moisture was falling. "This stuff comes up about as much as it comes down. An umbrella doesn't help. You should get a 60/40 coat."

"What's that?"

"Like this," she said, pulling on the front of her rain parka. "It sheds moisture, but it also breathes."

"Breathes?"

"Lets your body moisture out, you know?"

André frowned and pulled his suede jacket closer around his slim torso.

"Not very smart."

Julie shook her head. "Smart? Oh, you mean like fashionable. Well, leather really doesn't work in rain."

Zelda scampered ahead quickly, stepped to the side of the walk, and started turning a tight circle.

André pointed at her. "What's she doing?"

"That means she is going to poop," Julie said. She stopped while the dog hunched her back and took care of her business. Once she was finished, Zelda hopped away and stood, waiting.

Julie pulled a plastic bag over her hand and leaned down to pick up Zelda's pile.

"What are you doing?" André jumped back, disgusted.

"Cleaning up after her," Julie said, turning the bag inside out and tying it closed.

"You do that every time?"

"Of course. You can't just leave it there for someone to step in."

Julie handed André the leash and stepped over to a trash can and deposited Zelda's contribution. She looked back at André.

"You're not much of a dog person, are you?"

"I like dogs," he said, unconvincingly. He sounded like even he didn't believe it.

Julie retrieved the leash, and they returned to the path and headed toward the cliff overlooking the sound.

"How long do you have her?" André asked.

"Well, I wish it were forever. But she's a big dog. She'll probably only be with me another ten years."

"*Années?*"

"*Ouí. Années. Est-ce-que un problem?*"

"No. No," André said, hesitantly. "But when we go to France?"

"You mean to visit? I'm sure Jon will be happy to keep her."

Zelda pulled up to the spot on the cliff overlooking the water where they usually paused to take in the scenery and sat.

"Yes, to visit," André said, holding back a ways from the edge of the cliff. "But maybe later to live?"

Julie spun around. "You want to live there?"

"After a while. Don't you? I think you love France."

"Yeah, but not until Zelda is gone for sure." She shook her head. "We have a lot to talk about, André."

André grabbed her free hand and pulled her back to him. "Yes! We do," he said. "So much to talk about!" He leaned forward to kiss her, but Julie moved back toward Zelda. She squatted down and put her arm around her big dog.

"Don't listen to him, sweetie," she said, her mouth close to Zelda's ear. "I'm not leaving you again."

MONDAY MORNING, JULIE LED HER new assistant up and down the aisles in the wine store, pointing out its organization. "And here are our imports, organized by country. I've thought from time to time that perhaps we should organize them by varietal or by region. Most Americans choose wine by their preference for the grape or region, not by country."

"Oh, I agree," said Sara, a bit too enthusiastically. "It makes no sense by country. People don't come in and ask for a 'French wine,' do they? They say, I'm looking for a Burgundy."

Julie let Sara's sycophancy slide. She was undoubtedly trying to make a good impression as an agreeable and faithful employee from the start.

"Exactly," she said. "That's exactly what I'm saying. Or sometimes they'll say I want a mourvèdre, not knowing that a monastrell from Spain is the same grape but maybe just a different style."

They were interrupted by chimes at the door. Julie peered around the end of the aisle.

"André! What a surprise!" Julie sounded elated, she realized, but in fact, it was the surprise of seeing him that raised her voice.

Sara walked up behind her, and Julie turned sideways to introduce her.

"*Je suis enchante!*" André said, grasping Sara's hand and bending down to kiss it. "I am certain you will sell much wine for *ma cherie.*"

Julie caught herself rolling her eyes and stopped before André noticed. "Perhaps you can tell that André is from Paris," she said to Sara. "We met last summer when I was apprenticing there."

Sara, apparently enchanted as well, smiled sweetly, revealing deep dimples that transfixed her look from grown-up to cherublike.

"*Enchantee, aussi,*" she answered André.

Perhaps she'd do well with male customers, Julie thought, watching her. Julie herself had always preferred to help women choose wine. She had less patience with the flirtations of men.

She turned to André. "Why the surprise visit?"

André bounced on his toes, excited about something. "I know how much you like to plan ahead. I made a reservation for tomorrow night at Jon's restaurant. Will that be okay?"

"Ah, sure," Julie said. "I'll have to figure out what to do with Zelda. But that will be nice. I've never been to Bin 409."

"Why not?" he asked. "Is it not good?"

"No. It's supposed to be great. I just have never had a reason to go there. It's a little above my pay grade."

Sara jumped in. "It's great. I've been there a couple of times. Great wine list."

André winked at her but turned back to Julie. "So, it's a date?"

"Sure. I hope it is after seven. I don't close the store until then."

"Of course not. Earlier than eight *est barbare*. I can pick you up, no?"

"Sure. I just have to see if Jon can look after Zelda."

André frowned at the dog's name. "Oh, yes. Zelda. Yes, of course. Okay. I will leave you to work." He leaned forward for a kiss, and this time Julie let him meet her lips. He waved and skipped out the door.

"He seems genuinely infatuated with you," Sara said as they watched him turn down the sidewalk. "But I sense a bit of tension there?"

"You are very perceptive. I appreciate that. Perhaps I'll explain later." Julie shook her head sadly. "When I figure it out for myself."

That afternoon, after spending a few hours showing Sara the store, demonstrating the point-of-sale system, and going over store policies, Julie excused herself and slipped into the back room to get some bookkeeping done. As she sat in front of her computer, she pushed the speaker on her landline and dialed Jon.

"Hello?"

"Hi, Jon."

"Julie? What is this number?"

"It's the store. I'm in the back, working on updating the website, so I've got the phone on speaker."

"Oh."

Julie waited for Jon to continue, but he said nothing. Why the cold shoulder? she wondered.

"Are you there?" she asked.

"Yes. You called me. What do you want?"

Julie frowned. "Is something wrong?"

"I'm studying, Julie. What is it?"

Julie paused, wondering if it was a bad idea to call, but she continued. "I wanted to know if you're working tomorrow night."

"I always work Tuesday nights. Why?"

"I apparently need someone to watch Zelda, so I was just thinking if your schedule had changed…"

"You know it hasn't changed. I would have told you if it had. But is this going to be a habit with you now that André is here?"

"What do you mean?"

Jon snorted. "Well, I suppose you will be busy now. No time for Zelda."

"That's not true. It's just one night. One dinner. It won't be a habit. I can't afford it to be a habit."

"Perhaps André doesn't have the same restrictions."

Julie considered taking on the argument that Jon seemed interested in starting. But they had become such good friends. This change in his attitude was distressing.

"Yes, maybe not," she answered instead. "Well, sorry to bother you. How was your trip?"

"I'm sorry, Julie, but I've got to go." And with that, the phone went dead and the dial tone came back.

Julie stared at the phone for a minute before punching in another number.

"Hey, Jules," Cary answered. "What's up? I heard you found an assistant. Just in time."

"Yeah, I think Mom and Dad left this morning."

"They did. I took them to the marina. I've never seen them so excited."

"That's great."
"So, you called?"

Fourteen

Cary's long legs stretched all the way across the narrow deck that flanked the south side of the houseboat he rented on Lake Union. His eyes were closed, his hands relaxed and folded on his stomach as he soaked up the late-day sun on an old wooden bench that perfectly matched the gray siding behind him.

As Julie and Zelda stepped down the boardwalk toward him, Zelda pulled, anxious to greet her uncle, and Julie stopped to unhook his leash. The dog leapt forward, ran down the walk, and jumped up to hit the dreamy Cary on the chest.

"Whoa!" Cary jerked awake and fought to keep his balance on the bench. "What the … ." He sat up and shook off his surprise.

"Ah, how are you girl?" he said, wrapping his arms around the big dog.

"Hey," Julie said, catching up to Zelda.

"My god, she's not losing any weight, is she?" Cary asked.

"Not with two of us to spoil her." Julie sat down beside her brother.

"So, I hear André finally made it. When do I get to meet the lover boy?" Cary prodded.

"Yeah, well, we'll have to figure that out. Thanks for keeping Zelda. Can I pick her up in the morning? Our dinner reservation isn't until eight, so I'm guessing it will be dark down here by the time we're done."

"Sure," Cary said. Zelda quieted down and flopped onto his feet.

Julie sat closed-eyed, her face tipped up to the sun, frowning. She could feel Cary's eyes on her.

"Anything wrong, Julie? I thought I'd see you happy as a clam."

Julie blinked her eyes open and forced a smile. "Who says I'm not?"

Cary said nothing; his stare communicated his concern for her.

"Okay, you could always see right through me," she said. "But I'm not really sure what it is. I just feel a little confused right now."

She stood up and handed him Zelda's leash.

"Could it be—" Cary started, but Julie held out her palm.

"Please. Let's not talk about it now. I've got to get home and change. André is picking me up in a half hour." Julie saw Cary shaking his head, but she turned to leave, hurrying up the boardwalk, back to her car.

Cary called after her: "I think I have a pretty good idea what the problem is." Before she stepped off the walk, she heard him say to Zelda, "And I'll bet you do too."

As the limousine pulled up to the restaurant, Julie's

mood darkened. The prospect of Jon watching her and André together from his post at the bar saddened her more than it made her nervous. She didn't expect Jon to make a scene—or show any reaction at all. But she did worry that André might misbehave. Would he walk right up to Jon and beg for an audience with the chef?

The driver hopped out before Julie could find the door handle, and her passenger door popped open. He reached in to offer her his hand. André followed her out and up to the big door of Bin 409.

"Is there a problem, Julie?" André asked, reacting to her gloomy face.

"I'm not sure it's a good idea to come here," she said. "Jon knows you're interested in a job. Doesn't it look too obvious?"

André opened the door and took her arm, steering her inside. "What do you mean? Wouldn't you want to check out a restaurant where you might work? I need to see the menu, and see how things are prepared. I need to know something about the cuisine."

Julie nodded at his logic, but she couldn't force a smile. How miserable would the next couple of hours be?

The host greeted them and checked off their reservation on his tablet. He pulled two menus and a wine list off his desk. "This way, please."

He led them to the middle of the restaurant, and Julie avoided looking toward the bar. André pulled out the chair, and she tried to wave him off.

"Oh, that's not necessary," she said.

"Of course it is. Chivalry is not dead," he said, helping her pull the seat up to the table.

Julie sat and stole a glance around. Jon stood at the bar, but he was looking in the other direction and she breathed a sigh of relief. Perhaps he hadn't seen them come in. Maybe he'd not notice them at all as long as he stayed busy and

André did nothing to call attention to them.

"May I offer you a cocktail, madam?" The waiter interrupted her thoughts.

"Ah, sure. How about a glass of Prosecco?" she said, looking up into his fawning face.

"Oh, no, no, no!" André nearly shouted. "It must be Champagne. Give me a moment with the wine list, monsieur?"

Julie watched the waiter's expression change from obsequious to charmed. Apparently, he was impressed with André's accent. He bowed slightly and backed away to give André time to consider what bottle to order.

Julie looked over her menu as André perused the wine list. The waiter returned and André pointed. "A fine selection," the waiter said. They always say that, Julie thought.

"I hope you are not spending too much, André," she said. "I don't need to be spoiled, and you need to find a job. And chefs aren't paid here in Seattle like they are in New York."

"This is not your concern, *mi amor*. This is a special night."

"Our first date in this country?"

André smiled smugly. "Yes! That's it!" he said, leaving Julie with the impression that it wasn't it at all.

A GOOD NINETY MINUTES LATER, the waiter was removing their entrée plates, and Julie tried to stifle a yawn.

"Another bottle of the Champagne, *s'il vous plait?*" André looked up at the waiter.

"Oh, no, André," Julie pleaded. "I work tomorrow."

André spoke to the waiter. "Do not mind the lady. I insist."

"In no more than a moment," the waiter responded, walking away with his hands full of dishes.

Julie was beaten. There was no way she could convince

a man who was accustomed to occupying a dinner table until well after midnight that 10 p.m. was a respectable time to retire. She would have to try to catch up on sleep over the weekend.

"This has been an incredible night, André," she said, and in many ways, she meant it. André had behaved himself, leaving Jon alone at the bar. Her lamb chops were perfectly broiled and deliciously seasoned. The Champagne was the best she'd ever tasted on U.S. soil. "I haven't been so pampered since that night before I left Paris."

"Aw, but the night is not over!" André exclaimed, pointing to the waiter with a flourish of his arms.

The waiter approached with two ramekins of creme brulé. Immediately behind him, the sommelier arrived with an open bottle of Champagne and filled their glasses.

As the flurry continued in front of her, Julie looked up and saw Jon watching from the now-quiet bar. She had avoided meeting his eye all night. But now, her heart jumped at the sight of his placid expression. He saw them, but it appeared that he didn't care.

"I propose a toast to us," André said, raising his flute to get Julie's attention. "To our future."

She lifted her glass to his, but instead of drinking, André stood up and swiveled down to a knee beside her. Julie was confused for only a moment before it dawned on her. He was going to propose. Officially.

He pulled the little velvet box from his jacket pocket, opened it and held it out for Julie's inspection. It was, of course, a ring. She glanced at it and then back up at the bar. Jon was still watching, his face still blank, and she looked away.

"I am sorry I wasn't able to give you this before you left France," André was saying. "But this gives me a chance to ask you again. Julie DuChamps Bouvier, will you be my wife?"

Julie shot a glance at the bar. Jon wasn't there, and she turned back to André's expectant eyes. She hesitated, but she knew this wasn't the time nor the place to change her mind.

"Of course I will, André," she whispered. "Of course I will."

Fifteen

As Julie approached Cary's houseboat the next morning, he and Zelda were sitting in the same place she had found him the day before, enjoying second-day-in-a-row sunshine. This time, Cary was sipping from a large mug, and Zelda was the one snoozing.

As Julie's steps vibrated the planks of the houseboat deck, Zelda shook herself awake and sauntered over to greet her.

"Well, that's an unenthusiastic greeting," she reprimanded her dog. "What, you've decided that Cary's your favorite now?"

Cary grinned. "You seem chipper this morning," he said. "Want some coffee?"

"No, I have to get Zelda home and get to work," she said. She walked up to the bench and held out her left hand, showing off her new diamond.

Cary looked at it solemnly.

"Aren't you happy for me, Care Bear?" she asked, pulling her hand back.

Cary shook his head. "Are you sure?" he asked.

"Why wouldn't I be?"

Cary paused, looking as if he were parsing his words in his head before he spoke them. "Well, for one thing, he isn't particularly fond of Zelda. You told me that yourself."

"Maybe he just needs some time to get used to her. She can win anyone over. Everybody loves Zelda."

Cary patted the seat next to him.

"Sit down, Jules," he said.

Julie hesitated. She didn't want her positive attitude that morning—the first she'd had about André since he arrived—to be squelched by her brother. What? Was he jealous?

"Okay, out with it," she said. "What's your problem?"

"I saw what had happened between you and Jon," he answered quietly, sounding afraid to state anything too vociferously.

"Nothing was happening—"

Cary held up his hand to stop her. "No, hear me out."

Julie sat back and looked out over the lake. She'd better let him have his say now or something unresolved would sit between them.

"I've never seen you get that close to someone so quickly," Jon continued. "It was only a month and you were finishing each other's sentences. Your face lit up when he was around. You have to admit it. You feel something for him. A whole lot of something."

"What do you know about this?" Julie didn't want to think about Jon. It was time for her to move forward with her life, and her plan for months had been to do that with André.

"Well, I'm a guy," Cary said, chuckling at his own obvious observation, "and this much I can tell you. I've never seen a guy more smitten than Jon."

Julie closed her eyes and breathed deep. "Thank you very much for that information, brother. But I'm sorry. André came all the way to the U.S. to be with me. Jon just happened to live next door. You don't really fall in love with the boy next door except in the movies."

"Oh, but you *do* fall in love with the gorgeous Frenchman who swept you off your feet in Paris?" Cary laughed. "That sounds like a movie script to me."

Julie lifted her left hand and waved it in front of Cary again. "This says 'yes,'" she said. "André wouldn't have given this to me if he weren't 'smitten' with me too."

Cary paused and looked away. "Well, then I guess you're a very lucky girl," he said. "You get to choose between two smitten beaus."

"I already have. And as far as I know, Jon isn't even a choice."

"And what if he is?"

Julie signed deeply. "Care Bear. This isn't your problem. Wait until you meet André. You'll see how charming he is. Then you'll understand."

"I can't wait," Cary deadpanned.

Julie sat for a long minute, saying nothing. She didn't want to hear this. Thinking about Jon would only delay and complicate things. There was nothing wrong with marrying André, and nothing to gain from a relationship with Jon.

"I've got to get going, Jules," her brother interrupted her thoughts. "I've got a couple of interviews in Yakima with wineries. Thanks for making those contacts." He stood up and handed Julie Zelda's leash.

"Well, don't go mad," she said, standing up and leaning in to hug him.

"I'm not mad," Cary said unconvincingly. "I just need to get going." He scratched Zelda on the head and turned to walk into the houseboat.

"Come on, Zellie," Julie said, hooking up Zelda's leash to her collar. "I've got to get to work and you have to go visit your uncle Jon."

COMING IN THE FRONT OF the apartment building from work that evening, Julie scrounged in her purse for her keys and nearly ran into into Jon.

"Oh, hey!" she said. "Sorry. I should look where I'm going."

"Hello, Julie," Jon muttered. "I hear you're now formally engaged."

"Did you hear or see that?" she asked, eyeing him suspiciously. Had he seen André get down on his knee before disappearing from the bar the night before.

"See what? I have no idea what you're talking about. I talked with Cary today. He told me."

Julie held up her hand. "Yes. We are formally engaged," she said. "Now I have a wedding to plan at the same time I'm trying to train a new employee."

Jon smirked. "Yeah. Well, life is rough. But, hey. I just let Zelda in your apartment. We finished our walk. I've got to get to work."

"But it's Wednesday, your day off."

"I picked up an extra shift. Something to soak up my free time." He stepped around her.

Julie grabbed his arm as he passed. "Jon. I still want to be friends," she said, pleading. "Can't we? We still share Zelda. And we're neighbors. Can't we still walk Zelda together sometimes? Like we used to?"

Jon looked away, down the street, avoiding her eyes.

"Sure. Sure. Sure, we can. I'll give you a call sometime." He pulled away and strode out the door and down the sidewalk. Julie watched him go. Why was he making her so sad?

"Damn him," she said, unlocking her apartment door. "He has no right to try to ruin my happiness. Him or Cary."

A WEEK LATER, JULIE HAD found no time to think about a wedding. Teaching Sara what she needed to know, doing the bookkeeping, and managing the store took up every minute of her day; and making dinner and walking Zelda with André soaked up her evenings and the weekend. She was glad they hadn't set a date yet, as she didn't need the added pressure of a wedding deadline.

Updating her inventory on the computer on the counter, Julie heard the door chime and looked up to see André rushing in. Sara stepped aside as he scooted past her in the aisle.

"Julie! Julie!" he shouted. "You won't believe this." He stopped, breathless, and put his palms on the counter before her. She looked quizzically at him, and before she could ask him what was so exciting, he spat out his news. "I just got a call from Chef Luke Guillot in New York. Isn't that great? Can you believe it?"

"Who's that?" she asked, knowing her question risked his disdain.

André huffed, as she expected he would. "Only the best French chef in *Etas-Unis! Proprietaire de L'Escargot*! I can't believe you have not known of him!"

Julie smiled apologetically. "I'm kind of a West Coast girl, André. What goes on in New York is fairly peripheral to us here."

"But New York is not *secondaire*! In your country it is the capital of cuisine!" He waved his hands with enthusiasm.

"Well, I think there are those who would argue the point," Julie said softly. She saw Sara smile with amusement. "But what did Chef Guillot want?"

"He wants me to come to New York to interview for a position in his restaurant!"

Julie stared at André. Was he serious? He had just arrived in Seattle, and now he was heading to New York?

"Sara, if you need something we'll be in the back," Julie said. She motioned to André. "André, *avec moi.*"

As soon as he followed her into the back room, Julie turned and confronted him. "What are you talking about? We were going to get married. And now you want to move to New York?"

André grinned. Clearly, he wasn't reading her right. "You will come with me," he said. He was so excited he was bouncing on his toes. "We will get married there. All the best of America is in New York City!"

Julie took a deep breath to keep her temper from was flaring. "I don't know why you think that, but I certainly don't."

André finally picked up on her mood. "Please, Julie," he pleaded. "You must come with me to see. Let's see if there's a place for us there. This is the chance I want! The very best French restaurant in *le monde nouveau!*"

He stepped forward to grasp her shoulders, but she moved back.

"I don't know," she said. "My life is here. This is my store now. I'd have to leave Zelda behind. This makes no sense to me, André."

He lowered his voice and looked at her sweetly. "It makes sense because we are to be married," he said. He stepped toward her again and pulled her toward him. He kissed her lightly on the forehead. Julie turned away, folded her hands, and put her knuckles to her lips.

"André," she said. "The other day you told me you want to move back to France some day and you want me to come with you. Today you tell me we should move to New York so you can follow your dream. When were you going to ask me what I want?"

"But we want the same thing, Julie," he insisted. "To be married. You said yes. You said you wanted to be married, *oui?*"

"I do want to marry you, André."

She hesitated before continuing, wondering if that was still true. He'd slipped the ring on her finger only a few days before, and she hadn't slept well since. Backing out of an engagement would be one thing—hard enough—but moving all the way to New York and then deciding it was a mistake would be far worse. "I need some time to figure this out. To think it through. Can I have a couple of days?"

André walked around to face her and waved a long blue envelope in front of her face. "I thought you might need some time. So, these are for Thursday."

"What is that?"

"Airplane tickets. Two days from now. How is that?"

"So much for giving me time," she said sardonically. He just smiled at her brightly.

This was not going well, she thought. Not going well at all.

Sixteen

Julie cradled the phone on her shoulder as she bent over her suitcase and pulled on the sticky zipper.

"I'm glad you still have reception, Mom," she said. "How far up the coast have you sailed?"

"Oh, not far," her mom said. "We're taking our time. This is the first time in our lives we don't have to hurry. No deadlines! Can you imagine?"

"That's great. But, there's something I need to talk with you about."

"You're getting married."

Julie grabbed the phone in her hand and sat down on her bed. "So, who told you? Cary?"

"Yes, he called us a couple of days ago. I'm so sorry we didn't get to meet André before we left. But you're not in a hurry, are you? You won't get married before we get back."

"Of course not."

"Are you excited?"

"Well, something else has come up," Julie said. She paused before divulging the news of her trip to New York.

"But you're not planning to move there, are you?" Her mother's voice rose, and she didn't sound happy.

"Oh, no," Julie said. She planned to put off that decision as long as possible, and she didn't want to raise the issue until she had to.

"So, anyway, Cary is going to move into my apartment while I'm in New York so he can help Jon take care of Zelda. I guess things in Yakima didn't work out. He didn't get either of those jobs. The other thing is that Sara is leaving as soon as I get back. I liked her a lot, but she got a better offer. Cary's going to help her in the store too."

"Wow, you're depending a lot of that little brother of yours."

"I know," Julie said with a little chuckle. "Who would have guessed that would ever happen."

"Well, he's growing up," her mother said. "Finally."

"So, I'll be back in a week, and I'll start the search for an assistant all over again."

A loud knock on the door triggered Zelda's even louder barking.

"That's André at the door, Mom. He got a car to take us to the airport. Apparently, Chef Guillot is sparing no expense to get him there. I have to run."

"Okay, honey. Be careful. I love you. Dad too."

"I love you too," Julie said, pulling her suitcase off the bed. "Give Dad a kiss."

Julie hung up and pulled the bag to the door and out to the foyer.

"Quiet!" she ordered Zelda and opened the door. André stepped in and kissed her on the cheek. Zelda walked away, not waiting for a greeting from him. She plopped down at the other end of the living room and put her head down to pout.

"Could you wait right here for a minute?" Julie asked André. "I've got to take Zelda down to Jon's apartment. I'll be right back."

She picked up the leash, and Zelda jumped up and ran to her.

"Why didn't you do that earlier?" André asked.

"I wanted to spend as much time with her as I could." Julie ignored André's disapproving head shake. He plopped down on a chair and looked at his watch.

"Please hurry. The car is waiting."

JULIE SAT ON THE SQUARED-OFF chair in the first-class Alaska Airlines' lounge, pulled her roller bag close, and sank into the uncomfortable foam cushion. The fabric was scratchy on her legs, and she wondered if she should have worn pants instead of shorts. Airplanes could be over-cooled, especially in first class, where there were fewer bodies packed into the space. She hadn't flown on a domestic flight for so long, she didn't even know if the airlines supplied blankets anymore.

André had sat at one of the long counters provided as work spaces for passengers and pulled out his laptop as soon as they came in. Julie sat and watched planes taxi back and forth out on the tarmac. Why did they have to get here so early? she'd asked André when he was checking his big bag, but he shrugged her off. He seemed anxious—perhaps he was worried about the upcoming interview with Chef Guillot.

She left him alone after that, but it still bugged her to be separated from Zelda before she had to be, just so she could sit in this uncomfortable chair for the next two hours and watch André scroll through his Twitter account and emails.

She rose to check out the fruit buffet along the wall just as André's phone buzzed. He pulled it out of his pocket and glanced at the screen. "It's the chef. Could you watch my computer?" He pointed to the wall of windows overlooking the runways. "I'm going over there to get better reception."

With his phone to the ear, André sang a French greeting and walked away. Julie sat down at André's laptop. Already she felt like his lackey, his assistant. In the two weeks since he had arrived in Seattle, he seemed like an entirely different man than she'd known in Paris. There, he'd been fun and entertaining, eager to show off his hometown, and happy to spend lazy days with her at outdoor cafés and benches along the banks of the river, while she read classic 18th-century French writers who had never interested her before.

She glanced down as the screen of the laptop. André had been in the middle of a response to an email from Guillot's secretary:

There will be no problem with the green card. I get married soon and we have no problem with immigration. Plan is to

The email was unfinished. Reading it, Julie frowned. She looked up at André, standing with his nose practically touching the window pane, his back to her. She scrolled down to read the email that Guillot's secretary had sent to him.

We are very excited to talk with you about the position of sous chef here this week. However, we are concerned that you do not have a stable immigration status.Immigration is getting a lot stickier these days. Do you have plans to get a green card. How are your marriage plans coming? As we talked last week, marriage would solve the problem. Or are you applying for citizenship? Please get back to us asap. I'll send a limo to Newark for you. Bientot! Marie for Chef Guillot.

Julie looked away, perplexed. André had proposed marriage just before she left for Seattle. Was this his plan all along? To use her to cement his immigration status in the U.S.? Was she just convenient? She thought back to her time in Paris, remembering what she had tried so long to forget. For nearly a year, he had insisted their relationship wasn't exclusive, until, all of the sudden, just before she left France, it was. She'd wondered at the time what triggered his change of heart, but she put it out of her mind, believing his love simply had grown—and thinking she was lucky he had come to realize just in time that he didn't want to lose her.

Instead, she wondered now, had he realized just in time that she could be his ticket to New York?

As André put his phone back into his pocket and walked back to her, Julie stood up.

"I've been thinking, André," she said. "What if I move to New York, but we don't get married right away? You should be sure your job is going to work out before we take any more big steps, don't you think? Perhaps I should stay in Seattle until—"

"What?" André interrupted. "No, I just talked to the chef about this. We must get married. I cannot stay in Les Etas-Unis unless we get married."

Julie nodded and put her hand over her eyes. She took a deep breath before facing him again.

"Is that what this is about?" she asked, pointing to his laptop.

André cringed.

Julie held up her hand, holding the engagement ring right in front of his eyes. "This ring is all about you getting to stay in the United States? All about your plan?"

André stepped closer and put his hands on her shoulders. Julie noticed people had turned to watch them. She must have been talking too loud. Now they had an audience.

"No, no! I love you, Julie. I want to marry you because I love you," André insisted. Julie saw a woman directly behind him shake her head and roll her eyes. Apparently she wasn't convinced.

"You're wrong, André," she said, lowering her voice. "You want to get married because it's part of your plan. It's not about me. Everything we did back in Paris was just a setup, wasn't it?"

Julie's knees felt weak, and she turned to sit down on her uncomfortable chair. Tears stung in her eyes.

André flipped the lid down on his laptop and stood over her.

"I'm sorry you saw that email, Julie. It doesn't take away from the fact that I love you. I would want to marry you even if we weren't in *Etas-Unis*."

Julie blinked down the first stream of tears. She looked up at him angrily. "Can't you say 'United States?' Why is it always 'Etas-Unis?'" She knew her complaint was vapid. She wasn't one of those people who insisted that immigrants spoke English. She was tolerant, knowing how hard it was for her to learn a foreign language. But suddenly everything André had done over the past two weeks bugged her.

"I'm sorry. But what does—"

"André, it's just part of our problem," she interrupted. "I didn't realize until you got here that we are so different. In Paris, I was happy to fit into your life. I ate what you ate. I dressed the way your mother dressed. I spoke French. It was lovely. But here, you don't want to live like I do. You don't want to know Zelda. You don't want to stay in Seattle.

You haven't even asked to meet my brother, my best friend in the world."

André raised his eyebrows. "I thought I was your best friend."

"For a while, I did too," she said in a harsh whisper. "But I was wrong." She pulled the ring from her finger and held it out to him. He looked at it, and when it appeared she was about to drop it, he put his hand under it and caught it.

"This makes things so much more difficult," he said. He sighed deeply and looked away as his eyes reddened.

"For you, maybe," Julie said. "But I have a feeling you'll do just fine. You'll figure things out."

She stood up, extracted the rollerbag handle, and threw her purse over her shoulder.

"Goodbye, André," she said, wiping the last of her tears off her face. "And good luck. Now, I have to go see a man about a dog."

Seventeen

Settling into the back seat of a cab minutes later, Julie took her cellphone out of her purse and pulled up her speed dial. She punched in a number. Cary answered.

"Hi, it's me," she responded. "I'll be at the store in about a half hour."

Cary said nothing, and Julie could sense his confusion from miles away.

"Look, I'll explain when I get there," she said. "You're at the store, right?"

"Uh, yes. Me and Sara are here."

Julie stopped herself from correcting his grammar. This was no time to pull her big sister act. "And, Cary, when I get there, I'd like to talk with you."

"About what?"

Julie paused. She really wanted to wait until she could look him in the eye. But she plunged ahead.

"Would you consider coming to work at the store with

me? Permanently? Not as my assistant, but as a partner?"

Cary laughed so loud she had to pull the phone away from her ear. "What took you so long? I've been wait—"

"I know, I know," she butted in. "I don't know what took me so long to figure it out. But it makes sense, doesn't it?"

JULIE WAS MORE NERVOUS KNOCKING on Jon's door than she had been talking to Cary. She had screwed a lot of things up the past year and a half, and it was intimidating to try to fix them all at once. Especially when so much had changed in just the past hour.

Zelda barked inside, and Julie heard Jon admonish her, unconvincingly. So, he was far more of a pushover and far less of a disciplinarian than he tried to project, she thought, smiling.

The door opened, and Jon stood frozen for a couple of seconds, his eyes wide.

"Didn't you just leave?" he asked. "Won't you miss your flight?"

Julie squatted and petted Zelda. "Can I come in?"

Not waiting for an answer, she stepped into his apartment, Zelda by her side.

Jon closed the door behind her. "What are you doing here?"

Julie walked into his living room before turning around to face him. "Look, I'm sorry. I know I'm not the brightest person in this room—"

"No, Zelda is," he quipped.

Julie laughed, relieved. If Jon were really fed up with her, he wouldn't be making a joke.

"Yes, she probably is," she agreed. "But what I want to say is sometimes I don't see things that are right in front of my eyes."

Jon slipped past her and bent down to save something

on his laptop. "Like what?" he asked, standing up and facing her.

"Well. Like, I should have offered Cary the job at the store a long time ago."

Jon looked at her sideways. "You missed your flight to tell me this?"

"And especially …," Julie shook her head and paused. "Especially like I never really wanted to marry André. I fell in love with France, not with a particular Frenchman, and all it took for me to understand that was to see André here. He isn't part of my life here."

Jon stood, his expression blank as if he wasn't yet impressed with her epiphany.

"And I'm not who he thought I was either," Julie continued. "I'm not his rootless American girl, willing to move across the country and then across the ocean with him so he can live his dreams. I'm Julie from Seattle, owner of a wine store, mommy of Zelda."

She paused again, for a moment uncertain whether to go on. He nodded, and she breathed deep before continuing. "A woman who is in love with a man from Seattle. A man who is a daddy to Zelda."

Slowly, a smile grew across Jon's face. It tipped up on one side. "And who is this 'daddy to Zelda?'"

Julie stepped close and took hold of his shirt collar with both hands. Jon looked down into her eyes and put his hands on her waist. "You are sure about this?"

"Yes. I am absolutely sure."

Jon paused, his eyes searching hers. For what? Sincerity? Finally, he seemed to find what he was looking for and leaned forward, his lips meeting hers. Julie caught her breath. His lips seemed to be searching as hard as his eyes had for an answer. She tried to help him find it.

Their kiss was too much for Zelda. She ran out of patience, barking and bouncing on her front paws. Their lips parted and they reached down together to scratch her ears.

"Oh, Zelda, we love you too," Julie said.

"Yup. Everybody loves Zelda," Jon added.

Well, maybe not everybody, Julie thought. But everybody who matters.

She looked up, Jon looked down, and they picked up where they left off.

Author's Note

I started writing these novellas as screenplays about a month into the Covid-19 quarantine. I had passed the time that first month watching Hallmark Channel movies—something I had never done before. I found the films calming and mind-numbing in a good way. The formula was easy enough to parse, and Hallmark's guidelines are laid out clearly on its website: no violence and no sex. From watching, it was clear that swearing, religion, and politics were off-limits as well. Once I finished the screenplays, I turned them into these novellas. I imagine the readers most likely to enjoy this book will be those who enjoy Hallmark's romantic films. But even if you've never watched one in your life, I hope you find these stories calming and fun to read. Now that you've read Everyone Loves Zelda, try the other two: Love Between the Vines and Love on the Links.

About the Author

MARJORIE PINKERTON MILLER* IS THE romance pen name for Marj Charlier, author of contemporary and historical novels, two romance novels, and three romance novellas. Her first historical novel, *The Rebel Nun*, was published by Blackstone Publishing and won first-place prizes for historical fiction and overall fiction in the 2023 Colorado Independent Book Publishers Association EVVY awards. A former *Wall Street Journal* reporter, she holds degrees in journalism from Iowa State University and the University of Wisconsin-Madison, and an MBA from Regis University. She lives and works in Colorado Springs, CO, with her husband, the journalist Ben Miller.

*Pinkerton was the author's paternal grandmother's maiden name, and Miller was her mother's maiden name. Marjorie is her given name.